"I'd like to clarify a couple of points," Cam said, clearing his throat

He'd never realized how intimate his study could be. Maybe because he didn't usually bring a woman into it in the wee hours. Especially not a woman enjoying chocolate torte the way Deborah was. She didn't merely eat it. She savored it. Occasionally her eyes closed and an expression of pure bliss spread over her features.

"I would, too." Deborah seemed in no hurry, though. She took another bite of her cake. Hypnotized, Cam stared at her mouth. Right from the beginning, he'd noticed she had really great lips. Tonight they were off-the-scale great.

"But you go first." With a delicate sweep of her tongue, Deborah licked chocolate off her full lower lip.

Cam stifled a groan. How was he supposed to get this woman out of his thoughts when she sat there eating cake like...like...*that*?

This was impossible.

Dear Reader,

Happy New Year! Harlequin American Romance is
starting the year off with an irresistible lineup of four
great books, beginning with the latest installment in the
MAITLAND MATERNITY: TRIPLETS, QUADS & QUINTS
series. In *Quadruplets on the Doorstep* by Tina Leonard, a
handsome bachelor proposes a marriage of convenience
to a lovely nurse for the sake of four abandoned babies.

In Mindy Neff's *Preacher's In-Name-Only Wife*, another
wonderful book in her BACHELORS OF SHOTGUN RIDGE
series, a woman must marry to secure her inheritance, but
she hadn't counted on being an instant wife *and* mother
when her new husband unexpectedly receives custody of an
orphaned baby. Next, a brooding loner captivates a pregnant
single mom in *Pregnant and Incognito* by Pamela Browning.
These opposites have nothing in common—except an
intense attraction that neither is strong enough to deny.
Finally, Krista Thoren makes her Harlequin American
Romance debut with *High-Society Bachelor*, in which a
successful businessman and a pretty party planner decide
to outsmart their small town's matchmakers by pretending
to date.

Enjoy them all—and don't forget to come back again
next month when a special three-in-one volume,
The McCallum Quintuplets, featuring *New York Times*
bestselling author Kasey Michaels, Mindy Neff and
Mary Anne Wilson is waiting for you.

Wishing you happy reading,

Melissa Jeglinski
Associate Senior Editor
Harlequin American Romance

HIGH-SOCIETY BACHELOR
Krista Thoren

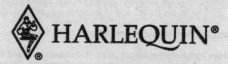

HARLEQUIN®

TORONTO • NEW YORK • LONDON
AMSTERDAM • PARIS • SYDNEY • HAMBURG
STOCKHOLM • ATHENS • TOKYO • MILAN • MADRID
PRAGUE • WARSAW • BUDAPEST • AUCKLAND

For Vikki Thoren
Wonderful person, loving sister, classy lady.

My thanks to Ann Leslie Tuttle for her
unfailing good humor and her superb, sensitive editing.

ISBN 0-373-16908-6

HIGH-SOCIETY BACHELOR

ABOUT THE AUTHOR

Krista Thoren grew up in Indiana. After ten years of college teaching, she now stays home with her toddler. She writes whenever possible, especially if the alternative is cleaning. Krista has too many hobbies and not nearly enough time. She lives near Chicago with her husband and daughter.

Books by Krista Thoren

HARLEQUIN AMERICAN ROMANCE
908—HIGH-SOCIETY BACHELOR

Dear Reader,

I'm happy to be writing for Harlequin American Romance. As both reader and writer, I enjoy books that feature a strong sense of community. In *High-Society Bachelor*, shop owners are friendly and loyal. Still, Deborah Clark and Cameron Lyle find that the community grapevine is more active than they'd like!

The idea for this book came largely from classic movies featuring elegant parties and sophisticated heroes. But I also wondered what would happen when a compassionate white lie backfired. My love of humor and fondness for cats combined to produce Libby, a cat with personality to spare.

I loved writing *High-Society Bachelor*, and I hope you'll have a great time reading it.

Best wishes,

Krista Thoren

Chapter One

"I expected more of a welcome from my girlfriend."

Deborah Clark stared at the man who leaned with nonchalant grace against the corridor wall outside her apartment. During the three months since she'd moved in above his office, Cameron Lyle had said about two dozen words to her, most of them brusque. Lofty and remote, that was him. Like Mount Everest, only not as warm.

And now he was making no sense.

"Your *what?*"

Then she remembered and drew in a sharp breath. *Uh-oh*. Her throat felt like something big and sharp had lodged in it.

Now she knew why he was here. This time it wasn't because her music was too loud, her cat too curious or her mail too abundant. No, this time it really was her fault.

The question was, how had he found out?

He crossed his arms and fixed a sharp green gaze on her. "My girlfriend." His polite tone and neutral expression gave her no clues as to his mood. His eyes showed a flicker of something that, in anyone else, she might have interpreted as humor. But in her ad-

mittedly limited experience of this man, he'd shown
no signs of having a sense of humor. Maybe someone
as good-looking and rich as he was never got the
chance to develop one.

Deborah forced her thoughts to a halt. "I can explain the whole thing," she said in her most cheerful
tone.

"You can?" He gave her that intense stare again,
the one that always made both her brain and her
mouth run amok. Which was silly, since it wasn't as
if she cared what he thought of her. Wealthy man-
about-town types didn't appeal to her.

Deborah nodded. "Yes. It's simple, really. In fact,
you wouldn't believe how simple it is." *Right, as in
simpleminded.* She couldn't believe it herself.

"Are you going to let me come in?" It wasn't really a question. At that moment, as if to underline his
demand, the door downstairs opened, sending an icy
blast of January air up the stairway.

"Come in?" She didn't want him in her apartment.
He was too big, too...male. But under the circum-
stances, she didn't have much choice. "Well, I guess
so, if it's necessary. But I'm sure we can settle this
very quickly, without taking too much of your time."
Or hers. She was running a tight deadline on arrangements for the Tyler twins' birthday party, and their
mother was not a calm woman.

"We need to talk." He brushed past her, and with
his six-foot-plus frame inside it, her apartment immediately shrank to shoebox size. His aftershave
smelled fresh and piney.

"Talk?" Deborah took a breath and forced herself
not to say anything else for five seconds. She wasn't
letting any man, especially one in pinstripes, turn her

into a parrot. The problem was, Cameron Lyle made every cell in her body go haywire. He always did. He'd stand and look at her without saying anything at all. He didn't smile much, either. The man should learn how to smile. It was, after all, a very natural thing to do, and it put people at ease.

But Cameron Lyle wouldn't know anything about that. And if he did, the idea of putting people at ease probably wouldn't be a selling point.

Deborah pointed to the couch. "Have a seat. Are you allergic to cats?"

He raised one dark brow. Now *that* he did well. It was obvious that he disapproved of not only her music, but practically everything else about her, too. She'd gotten a lot of brow action from him over the past three months. He had strong, very masculine brows to go with a strong, very masculine face. And his jaw was way more aggressive than any jaw she would consider going out with.

Deborah grimaced. She didn't want to guess where that thought had come from. It wasn't as if she even *liked* the man, for heaven's sake. He was the only person she knew who consistently challenged her natural optimism and good humor.

Still, he had to have a good side to him somewhere. After all, he attracted an amazing number of women. How many times had she gone downstairs to chat with his assistant, Barb, and found some glamorous woman waiting for him?

"No," said Cameron finally, settling himself onto her couch.

Deborah sat down in the armchair opposite the sofa and tried to remember what he was saying *no* about. "Cat hair," she explained after a moment. "Cat dander, to be more accurate. Libby sheds, and the hair doesn't always vacuum up completely. So it's a good thing you're not allergic. Now, let me tell you how this boyfriend-girlfriend thing came about.'' She took a long, steadying breath. ''Actually, I never used the word *boyfriend* to Marilyn. I just said I'd been seeing someone, and she asked who, and I said you.''

''I see.''

What that meant, and what exactly he saw, was a mystery to Deborah. His face gave nothing away. But based on all her other encounters with Cameron Lyle, disapproval had to figure in there somewhere.

''Strictly speaking, I do see you from time to time,'' she pointed out, trying not to sound as defensive as she felt. ''But of course Marilyn drew her own conclusions.'' *Which I did nothing to correct.*

She wanted to clear her throat, but that would make her sound as nervous as she was. Instead she traced a pattern on the arm of her chair. So much for telling herself that Cameron would never find out about her little misrepresentation, and that even if he did, he dated so many women he wouldn't notice one more in the crowd.

Wrong on both counts.

Deborah stifled a sigh. It would be nice if he would stop looking at her as if she were a zoo exhibit. His gaze was too intense. It made her feel completely off-balance. Plus, using the word ''boyfriend'' in connection with the man seated opposite her went beyond weird. Not only were they an unlikely pair, but there was nothing boyish about him. He was all lean muscle and hard edges.

In short, all man.

Which, of course, she had noticed even when she had been engaged to Marilyn's son, Mark.

His gaze held steady on her face. ''I'll admit I'm curious as to why you didn't use your fiancé if you needed to claim a boyfriend. I'd have thought he would be the ultimate in convenience.''

Deborah blinked. Aside from those two sentences being the longest ones he'd ever sent in her direction, he was apparently the only person in this little corner of Indianapolis who hadn't heard the news.

The interest her broken engagement had generated in Tulip Tree Square had taken Deborah totally by surprise, but as her friend Ann had pointed out, their small community of shop owners was closely knit, and people had to talk about something. If they didn't care about sports, then love lives were a decent alternative.

Tulip Tree Square needed more sports fans.

''I don't have a fiancé,'' Deborah said.

His brows shot up, but not in a supercilious way this time. He looked genuinely surprised. In his eyes she saw a quick flash of something else, too, something undefinable, before his gaze dropped to her left hand. For the first time since her breakup, Deborah was acutely conscious of her bare ring finger.

''No fiancé,'' he murmured.

''Right. Not anymore. Mark broke it off a month ago. And his mother was so concerned about me that I had to say something to reassure her. We had lunch together, except she wasn't eating any of hers, and she badly needs to get her strength back after her surgery—''

Deborah stopped. She simply *had* to control herself. She had to ignore his intense eyes and her own embarrassment and remember that this man didn't care two hoots about Marilyn not eating any of her roast beef au jus sandwich. Or that she'd been like an extra mother to Deborah for years. There wasn't much Deborah wouldn't do for Marilyn. A little white lie hadn't seemed too terrible if it brought her peace of mind.

"His mother. I suppose that would be Marilyn Snyder," observed the lofty Mr. Lyle.

"Right." Her own mother's best friend. Now that her mom had remarried and moved to Florida, it was up to Deborah to keep an affectionate eye on Marilyn during her convalescence. "You know her, obviously," Deborah added.

"Only slightly. Committee work."

She nodded. "Well anyway, Marilyn had an emergency appendectomy a few weeks ago. Unfortunately, her appendix exploded on the operating table, and the infection got really nasty."

He winced. "I see." He looked like he wished he didn't. "I had no idea she had a son. She didn't mention him to me at all during our conversation."

Deborah lifted one shoulder. "Well, since she thinks you're my new boyfriend—which, as I'll repeat, is *not* what I told her—she probably decided against mentioning an ex-fiancé. Besides, Marilyn hasn't been too thrilled with Mark lately."

That was an understatement. When Mark had broken off their engagement, his mother had been crushed. Deborah's mother hadn't turned any handsprings, either, because she and Marilyn had decided years ago that Deborah and Mark would make a perfect couple. The two mothers had been a lot more upset about the breakup than Deborah had been. Which, in the end, had told them all a lot.

She and Mark were both lucky to have escaped marriage. After all, Mark couldn't even decide which graduate degree to go for. He was obviously not ready to commit to any woman. And in the days following their breakup, Deborah had realized he wasn't the man for her.

All things considered, the two of them were lucky their mothers had given up gracefully.

But there was no point in going into details. Even if Cameron Lyle were interested, which he wouldn't be, it was none of his business.

"Marilyn's clearly a big fan of yours," he said. "Wanted to let me know how happy she is that you're having some fun these days."

Deborah stifled a groan. Marilyn, sweetheart that she was, had said those very words to Deborah, but somehow, coming from beautifully chiseled masculine lips, they sounded a lot less innocent.

"So tell me," he said. "Exactly what kind of fun are we having?"

She stared at the strong curve of his mouth. It tilted up a smidgen at the corners. Not a smile, but it wasn't a frown, either, so apparently he wasn't mad at her. He sounded curious, more than anything else. Curious and intrigued. Deborah met his interested stare and felt her pulse pick up speed.

"Well?" he prompted. "Are we talking generic, G-rated fun, here? Or a more interesting kind of fun?"

All sorts of images popped into her head, and not a single one was G-rated. Her face felt hot. "I don't think I specified," she muttered.

"I see." He watched her. "She also wanted to make sure I appreciated you."

Oh, boy. What in the world had he said to that? Maybe nothing. Hopefully nothing. After all, this was not a man who chatted.

His eyes held a gleam. "I assured her I appreciate you very much."

Deborah's pulse thudded faster still, but she ignored it. Probably just shock. Cameron Lyle obviously wasn't himself today, but tomorrow he'd give her the familiar stiff nod and everything would be back to normal. This was no time to be thinking that he looked like a human being this afternoon. A very attractive man, in fact, in spite of the ultraconservative and downright boring three-piece navy pinstriped suit he was wearing.

"After all," he continued, "it was clear that you were the one who told her we were involved, so I decided you must have a reason for this idiocy."

Scratch that last thought. He was not a human being.

Deborah counted to ten. He *had* helped her out by not giving her away to Marilyn. So what if Mr. High Society was a snob and considered the idea of dating her ridiculous? She wasn't lining up to go out with him and his jaw, either.

He still watched her closely. "Why did you pick me?"

"I didn't pick you!" She took a calming breath. "Well, I picked your name, that's true. But only because Marilyn wanted to know who the guy was. Like I said, at first I just told her I was seeing somebody. You know, somebody tall, dark and handsome." Deborah felt her cheeks warm. Why had she said that?

A skeptical little smile appeared at the corners of his lips. "And then my name popped into your head?"

"*No.*" She shifted. "Well, yes, actually, it did. Why shouldn't it? I pass by your sign downstairs at least six times a day. Cameron Lyle, M.B.A., Financial Consultant." And, of course, he fit the tall, dark and handsome description, although handsome was too bland a word to describe his aggressively attractive face and body.

However, his looks were completely irrelevant. She had *not* been thinking of Cameron Lyle, the man. In fact, she hadn't been thinking at all, because otherwise she'd have realized that Marilyn, a businesswoman herself, would have heard of him. And even though she'd never figured Marilyn would say anything, using his name had been dumb.

But then, impulses often turned out to be dumb, which was why she was trying to stop having them.

He leaned forward, his gaze sweeping over her face and body in leisurely passes. "You know, you should have dropped me a few hints. Why play games? We're both free, and I like admiration as much as the next guy. I'm sure we could arrange something—"

"*Arrange something?* I don't want—" Deborah saw his face and stopped. The crinkles around his dark green eyes gave him away, despite his deadpan expression.

He was laughing at her.

With anyone else, she'd have gotten a chuckle out of it, too. She liked to laugh, and she appreciated a good joke, even when it was on her.

But besides laughing at her, Mr. High Society was patronizing her. Every time he talked to her, she read dismissal in his eyes. It was all too obvious he saw her as an unsophisticated and naïve girl, instead of as the mature woman she really was.

"Very amusing," she muttered. It just went to show he wasn't always humorless and unfriendly. Sometimes he was humorless, unfriendly and sarcastic.

Deborah plucked a piece of lint from her royal blue leggings. Well, that wasn't quite true. Okay, so the man did have a sense of humor. She could acknowledge that fact, even though the discovery of it completely stunned her and his humor was unkind and came at her expense.

Still, Cameron Lyle should be careful, because an even less sophisticated woman than she was might think he'd been flirting with her just now. Which of course he hadn't been. After all, this was the man who drove a sleek, expensive car and had recently made *Indianapolis Living*'s "Most Eligible Bachelors" list. Not that she read columns like those, but from the moment she'd moved into the apartment directly over his large office, she'd gotten an earful from several interested parties in Tulip Tree Square, all of them female.

So she knew enough about Cameron Lyle's love life to realize that she was the total opposite of the women he dated. They were all sophisticated and impeccably stylish. Probably petite, too, and ultrafeminine.

All things she would never be. Things she would never *want* to be.

Deborah got up from her chair. "So that's the situation. A bit of a mess, I know, but it's only temporary. I apologize for any inconvenience..." She let her sentence trail off because it sounded uncomfortably like a renovation notice in a department store.

His dark head tilted. "I accept your apology, but that's not the main reason I came to talk to you."

"It isn't?" How could they have anything else to talk about? They had nothing in common. He spent his days in stiff business suits doing boring paperwork while she spent hers in comfy leggings planning cheerful kids' parties. In the evenings he ate elegant catered meals and escorted beautiful women to social engagements while she ate frozen dinners and read.

Lengthy, deep conversations between the two of them were not even a remote possibility.

"I want to hire you," he said.

Deborah stared. For a moment, that was all she could do, because although a variety of thoughts leaped into her head every time she saw the handsome and remote Mr. Lyle, none of those thoughts had anything to do with dinosaur birthday cakes, pizza parties or clowns.

He had to be kidding.

On the other hand, he looked serious, like someone ready to talk business. And it wasn't entirely impossible that he could need her company's services.

Even confirmed bachelors had nieces and nephews.

Deborah cleared her throat. "You want to hire me? To organize a party?"

"Yes."

She considered the idea, turning it around in her mind with the caution of someone tasting a food of unknown character. The difference was that in this case, she had enough knowledge to make her suspect that planning a party for Cameron Lyle would be a mistake. Accepting him as a client was a risk she shouldn't take. After all, sooner or later she'd have to say something to him. Then he'd give her one of those brusque, stuck-up, disapproving replies, and she would tell him to go soak his haughty head, and then—

"Will you do it?" he asked, saving her imagination any more work.

She opened her mouth to say "no" and then remembered that Libby's vet bill was due in less than two weeks. "Maybe. I'd need some details first." Deborah snagged a pen and some paper from the coffee table and gave him her best businesslike voice. "How old are the children?"

He frowned. "The children? There aren't—"

"Age group is the biggest factor, you know. It determines everything, from food to games. After all, we can't have twelve-year-olds playing pin the tail on the donkey, can we?" Mentally Deborah winced. She sounded like a geriatric nurse. And one look at his face told her he was completely lost.

"Is there a wide age range?" she asked. Actually, that was only a minor problem, but many clients were stumped by it.

He chuckled, and Deborah stared. She hadn't been positive the guy ever laughed, and she would never have guessed he could produce such an attractive sound. Deep, rich and melodic, it made her want to join in, even though she had no idea what was funny.

"Very wide," he agreed. "But I'm not hiring you for a kids' party."

Deborah frowned. "You're not? But that's what I do. Well, except for a few weddings—" She drew in a sharp breath and almost choked. "You're hiring me to plan your wedding reception?"

Good grief, no one on the block was going to believe this. She couldn't believe it herself, after all the what-a-hunk-but-he's-allergic-to-marriage sighing and sobbing she'd heard since she moved in. Just how everyone knew, or thought they knew, that he'd never marry was a mystery to her. Had he taken out a billboard ad?

More to the point, how had he sneaked a fiancée past the grapevine groupies?

"No, no," Cameron Lyle said, with a haste that made her want to laugh. "No reception. No wedding. I'm not getting married." He looked horrified, as if they were discussing a fatal disease.

Deborah felt a smile tug at the corners of her lips. Besides amusement, there was relief, pure and simple. With the exception of one last booking in March, and her own wedding, sometime in the distant future when she was very, very positive that her fiancé wasn't going to jilt her, she hoped to plan no more weddings as long as she lived.

"Fine, you're not getting married," she agreed. "And you're not having a kids' party. So what kind of event are we talking about?"

"A dinner party. A dinner dance, in fact. January thirtieth, seven-thirty. Sixty people, mostly business acquaintances." He ticked off the details with the air of someone who knew what he was doing and was never indecisive. "Something simple but elegant. Hors d'oeuvre, buffet service, dessert trays. Modern but conservative décor, probably silver and burgundy."

Deborah blinked. "And you want me to plan the event?" Assuming there was any planning left to be done.

"Right. Is there a problem with that?" he asked.

She thought about it. "Probably not." He had just handed her a golden opportunity, because this party sounded like exactly the type of event she wanted to specialize in. And since she'd been trying, so far unsuccessfully, to take her business in that direction, she shouldn't look a gift horse in the mouth. Still...

"Why?" Deborah asked, unable to stop herself. "Why are you asking me, I mean?"

For a second he looked like he was going to say something, but then he raised a brow instead. "Why shouldn't I?"

She could think of several reasons. Every time they met she got the impression he thought she was too talkative, too casual, too flippant, too unsophisticated and a whole lot of other *toos*. Of course, she herself knew that wasn't true, but then she wasn't him—a certified Type A personality who took himself and life way too seriously. Compared to him, she was downright frivolous.

"You don't know my work," Deborah pointed out. "For all you know, my event décor features plastic fruit, fringed table cloths and doilies."

"You don't seem like the doily type," he said. "In any case, I'll have final approval over everything."

Not exactly a strong vote of confidence. But it didn't matter. She really couldn't afford to turn down this opportunity.

"Okay, I'll do it," Deborah said. She told him her fee percentage and, when he nodded, she added, "Once we hash out the details, I'll write you up a proposal. I've also got a contract we can fill out."

"Good." He looked satisfied rather than surprised, but before Deborah could decide whether or not she was annoyed that he'd apparently been so sure she would be available to plan the event, he held up a hand. "Oh, yes. I'll need one other thing."

"What's that?" she asked.

"A hostess for my party."

Deborah frowned. "That's not part of the normal service."

"I realize that, but you can do it for me, can't you?" He gave her a confident smile that told her he fully expected her to agree.

Deborah eyed him without enthusiasm. She should have known that coming to a business agreement with this man wouldn't be easy. Most clients were more than satisfied if she threw in a free cake or pizza with the deal, but not him. Oh, no. Nothing so simple for him. He expected her to come up with a hostess for his party. Not an easy task.

And his confident smile made her want to grit her teeth. He probably used that smile on women all the time. It probably worked, too.

Well, it wouldn't work on her.

"I can throw in a server with the deal, but that's the best I can do," she told him finally.

He gave her a small, amused smile. "I'm not asking for this as a freebie in a business negotiation. I'm asking for it because you owe me a favor."

Deborah looked up at him. He had her there. "Yes, I suppose I do. Okay, I'll find you a hostess—"

"No." He shook his head. "I told you, this isn't a business issue. I'm asking for a personal favor."

Deborah met his gaze and then, suddenly, light dawned. She felt herself flush. He must think she was a complete idiot to be so slow catching on. Her only excuse was that this had to be the worst idea she'd heard in a long time.

"Wait a minute. You're not suggesting *I*..." She couldn't finish. The thought was too awful.

"Yes, I am," said Cameron Lyle. "I want you to be my hostess."

Chapter Two

Deborah did not look happy. That fact alone was noteworthy, since Cameron hadn't seen her any other way in the short time he'd known her.

During that time she'd met each of his complaints with a cheerful calm and a chatty reply that kept him off-balance. Amused, too, in spite of his irritation. Even during the past month, when she'd apparently been recovering from her fiancé's rejection, Cam would never have guessed it by seeing or talking to her. When their paths crossed, she was often deep in conversation with a neighbor, gesturing with an enthusiasm that echoed in her lively blue eyes. She always seemed about to smile.

Except for right now. Right now she looked like she'd rather be doing anything else than having this conversation.

"No." She shoved a hand through her thick blond hair. "I can't be your hostess."

Cam blinked. He wasn't prepared for a refusal at all, let alone such an abrupt one. What was the matter with her?

He gave a mental shrug. He couldn't afford to wonder what Deborah's problem was. He needed her, and she owed him her cooperation. Simple as that.

"This works out well," Cam said, ignoring her last statement. "I thought I was going to have to go without a hostess for my party, but that little problem is solved now that I've suddenly acquired a girlfriend." He put emphasis on the last few words.

Her expression told him she'd gotten his point, but Deborah shook her head. "I can't be your hostess," she repeated. "And I can't imagine why you'd want me to, anyway, since it's obvious you don't approve of me." Her gaze met his squarely, daring him to deny it.

Cam frowned. "What are you talking about?"

She snorted. "Frowns just like the one you're wearing now, that's what I'm talking about. I know disapproval when I see it, and that's about all I've seen from you, ever since I met you."

Cam stared at her. She was refreshingly honest. He ought to be able to return her honesty. He wanted to. But what could he say? *Yeah, you're right. I sure as hell disapproved of that engagement ring you were wearing. And I still disapprove of the ten years, minimum, difference in our ages.*

No, he couldn't say that. She would think he was chasing her, which couldn't be further from the truth. After all, even without the age gap they were completely incompatible. And yet he was relieved—happy, even—to see the last of that damned ring.

He couldn't explain what he didn't understand himself.

Cam settled for a small slice of the truth. "That wasn't disapproval. It was plain bad temper, and I've been meaning to apologize for it. Let's just say something was bothering me and leave it at that.''

She looked stunned. Her eyes were wide, almost swallowing up her extremely innocent-looking face. ''Okay,'' she said finally. After another long pause she added, ''But I still can't be your hostess.'' This time her voice held some regret.

''Yes, you can. Helping me out is the least you can do.'' He fixed her with a long stare. ''You owe me.''

She closed her eyes.

''Consider it a routine payment of a debt,'' he advised, watching despair fill her expressive features. He smiled. Talk about melodrama. She had an obvious flair for it. And he should know, because he'd had enough drama from women to last him a lifetime.

''I don't get it.'' She opened her eyes again and gave him a look that was both exasperated and uncomprehending. ''You've got tons of women to choose from. Why would you want me to hostess your party? People will think we're...you know...together.'' She waved a hand, making her aversion to the idea clear. But then she must have realized her response wasn't flattering, because her cheeks pinkened.

''Like Marilyn does, for instance?'' Cam asked with exaggerated politeness.

She shot him a quelling look. ''I told you, that was a spur-of-the-moment impulse. One little slip doesn't justify a larger deception. Anyway, as you yourself pointed out, the idea of us as a couple is implausible and *idiotic*.''

''I didn't say it was implausible,'' he argued. He wouldn't have said that, because it wasn't. Plenty of guys dated much younger girls. He just wasn't one of them.

"And the only reason we find ourselves in an idiotic situation is that you didn't give me a heads-up. You're lucky I didn't blow it," Cam told her. In fact, he'd come close to it. But he'd recovered in time. Stunned as he was, he'd also found himself more intrigued than he'd been in a long time.

Much as he hated to admit it, he'd jumped at the excuse to go challenge her for an explanation.

Deborah's head was bent as she examined her nails, which were perfectly groomed. Unvarnished and natural, like the girl herself. Then she looked up again. "You're right. Thanks for not giving me away."

"You're welcome." Cam eyed her mouth. She had a full lower lip that contributed a hint of sensuality to her fresh, girl-next-door good looks. He dragged his gaze away. She didn't seem exactly crushed about her broken engagement. Was that another example of her refusal to take anything in life seriously? Or was it only pretense, an attempt at salvaging her pride? Either explanation seemed plausible, but only one explained the story she'd told Marilyn.

"For what it's worth, I understand why you lied about having a boyfriend," Cam told her.

She grimaced. "I prefer the word *fibbed*."

"Fine. I know why you fibbed."

She sent him a wary look that didn't quite come off on a face as open and friendly as hers. "You do?"

"Sure." He shrugged. "Her son ditched you and you looked for a face-saver. It's a natural enough response. Egos are fragile things."

That earned him a scowl that looked even stranger

on her face. "First off, Mark did not 'ditch' me, at least not the way you make it sound. He's too civilized for that. Second, my ego is sturdy enough, thank you very much. As I said, I was trying to put Marilyn's mind to rest."

Irritated that she wouldn't come clean with him, Cam shot her a skeptical look. "Your ex-fiancé's mother? Uh-huh. I'm sure the fact that what's-his-name, your ex, would hear about your new boyfriend had nothing to do with it." Why had he said that? He felt ridiculous, as if they were college kids arguing over Sunday night pizza.

He, at least, had left his college days far behind.

"That's right, it had absolutely nothing to do with it." She looked like she actually believed what she was saying. Her deep blue eyes were wide and indignant. Truthful.

"It doesn't matter," Cam said finally. "You're better off without him, anyway. Don't the surveys say single women are happier than married women?" Barb kept up on all the surveys, and she didn't believe in sparing him any of the good news. The rest of the survey had claimed that married men were happier than single men.

He could still hear the triumph in Barb's voice, but Cam knew the survey was wrong on that point. It was wrong for the simple reason that men were biologically predisposed to prefer variety. They had a natural instinct to run from entanglement. Marriage was only for those who'd lost the energy to run.

He planned to stay energetic for life.

Besides, he'd seen no evidence of marriage producing long-term happiness for either men or women. At best they tolerated each other and at worst, they ended up in bitter custody battles over children who could only sit there in misery, wanting to be anywhere but there, in the middle of all the shouting.

The phone rang. When Deborah excused herself to go get it, Cam found himself disappointed. Based on her track record, her facial expression and her long silence, he figured she'd probably had something memorable to say. And now he'd miss it. His encounters with Deborah always left him strangely invigorated, as if he were a newly revved-up engine.

Cam took advantage of her absence to glance around her living room. Except for the couch he was sitting on, the furniture was wicker, which wasn't a favorite of his. It looked okay in this room, though, especially combined with lots of plants and a collection of brightly colored pillows. Two end tables painted with funky designs flanked the couch. The scarcity of furniture made him suspect that Deborah's apartment had been furnished on a tight budget. But she'd done a creative job of it. The best features of the room were the large stone fireplace and the hardwood floors.

He could hear Deborah's voice, a distant murmur as she talked on the phone in the kitchen. She had a clear, pleasant voice that suited her. Books and other collectibles told a lot about a person, so he got up and went over to look at her bookshelves.

She had political thrillers, which was a surprise. He recognized a couple of his own favorite authors. A few mystery novels, some romantic comedies and a variety of nonfiction titles rounded out her reading collection. There were several photographs of a teenage Deborah with another girl. Her sister? Probably, judging by the family resemblance. Nearby was another photo of a woman who had to be her mother. There was no evidence of her father.

Cam had just put the silver-framed photo down when Deborah strode back into the room, a tablet of paper in hand.

He liked the way she moved. It was one of the first things he'd noticed about her. She had a carefree, swingy kind of walk and the height to carry it off gracefully. She had to be five feet ten or so, with a slender, athletic build. Curves in all the right places. Dressed more classically, she would look elegant, but even in artsy clothes she was striking. Her bright blue tunic sweater and leggings accentuated her mile-long legs.

Even though Deborah Clark was way too young for him, he enjoyed looking at her. As he'd assured himself several times, there was nothing wrong with that. But it bothered him a little to realize that he especially enjoyed looking at her now that he didn't have to remind himself she was engaged, and he didn't have to feel the familiar and illogical surge of irritation that the reminder always carried with it.

The fact was that right from the beginning, he'd found it all too easy to watch Deborah. Her shapely body and streaky blond hair were eye-catching enough, but the lively intelligence in her eyes and the humor in her expression riveted his attention. Looking at her almost made him forget her flippant attitude, extreme chattiness and appalling taste in music. One thing was for sure: He would not be putting her in charge of the string quartet.

In fact, he'd have to keep her on a tight leash with every aspect of the party planning, because although she wasn't the doily type, tie-dye might not be far off the mark, and he wasn't a fan of the neo-sixties look. He'd agreed to offer the planning job to Deborah based only on Barb's assurances that the younger woman could produce elegant parties. His motherly administrative assistant had apparently added Deborah Clark to her collection of strays.

Cam watched as Deborah finished jotting something down on her small pad of paper. A favor to Barb was one thing, but he was no martyr. Fortunately, and thanks to Deborah herself, he would reap the added benefit of a hostess for his party. An attractive one, too. Deborah might not fit his image of the ideal girlfriend, but she was easy on the eyes. Most importantly, she wasn't going to make any demands on him during the evening. No expectations, no fits of fury, no sulking episodes. He'd be faced only with a cheerful, chatty female who would help him persuade little Heather Manders to exercise her teenage feminine wiles on someone else.

"Sorry about the interruption," Deborah said, looking up from her pad of paper. "But I always answer the phone during business hours since my company is home-based."

He nodded and focused his attention on the small, gray-striped cat that trotted behind her into the living room. "There's a familiar face," he commented, aware of mixed feelings. Although highly appealing, the animal reminded him of behavior he'd rather forget.

A month ago, the cat had followed Cam from the hallway into his office, where the feline had promptly curled up on his desk and fallen asleep on a stack of legal documents, wrinkling the top one beyond redemption. When Barb had identified the cat, Cam had stalked upstairs to deliver the interloper, along with a few curt words he shouldn't have come out with.

It was true that the wrinkled original contract had to be completely redone. It was also true that a robe-clad Deborah had arrived at the door looking damp and tousled, with an innocent gaze that didn't match her clothing. Still, Cam should have been polite.

Furthermore, he didn't want to analyze why so much of his annoyance with this girl seemed to have disappeared along with her engagement ring. Nothing about his reaction to her made any sense.

Was she even twenty-one?

"That's Libby. I think she remembers you, too," Deborah said now, as the cat twined herself around his ankles before jumping up into the wicker chair opposite the couch. The feline immediately settled into the cushions and went to sleep.

"Interesting name for a cat," Cam observed.

"I named her after my roommate," Deborah explained. "When Beth moved out, I replaced her with a cat. Sort of. Libby talks less and has a lot less energy than Beth, but she's good company." She turned back to look at Cam, and the dangly silver earrings she wore swung gently. "Let's see, where were we?"

"We were discussing the fact that you owe it to me to hostess my party."

She grimaced. "Okay. I agree I owe you one, but there must be some other way I can pay my debt." She gave him a hopeful look. "I could walk your dog for a week."

"I don't have a dog," Cam told her.

"Figures," she muttered.

"Look, why don't you clue me in?" He steered her over to the couch, and she sat down without protesting. "What's so terrible about hostessing my party?"

Aside from the fact that being romantically linked with him horrified her so much she'd rather take her chances with a dog. Cam grimaced.

Looking on the bright side, this situation was a nice change from being chased for his money. It was pretty damned ridiculous to be annoyed, especially since she wasn't an appropriate romantic interest for him, anyway.

For a long moment, it looked like Deborah was going to refuse to tell him anything. She sat there watching him with her big blue eyes. Finally, she gave a small shrug. "I don't like parties."

Cam stared at her. "But you plan parties. That's what you do for a living."

"Of course it is. That doesn't mean I have to like going to them," she explained, as if her line of reasoning made complete sense. His disbelief must have shown, because she sighed and continued. "I like the *idea* of parties, and I have fun planning them. I even enjoy the atmosphere if I'm working at an event. But going to a party, not having anything to do there, not knowing what to say—" She shook her head. "It's the pits." Her expression was eloquent.

"But you're so talkative," Cam protested. "You're a natural party girl."

She glared at him.

"I didn't mean it like that," he said.

"Don't call me a girl, either," she ordered. "I'm a woman."

He laughed.

Her glare intensified.

"Fine, you're a woman," Cam agreed. "A woman

who, every time I see her, is chatting away to some-one." Not to him, of course. She didn't chat with him. Probably because she didn't like him. Perfectly logi-cal, of course, since he hadn't been very nice to her. In any case, she didn't have to like him. She only had to agree to his plan.

"I like talking one-on-one," she said. "But I don't like crowds of people, all of whom I'm expected to exchange meaningless chitchat with." She gave him a determined look. "So let's just agree that I'd be a disaster as your hostess."

He shook his head. "I don't agree. You'll do fine." She would, too. It was only a party. They didn't need to have anything in common in order to spend one evening together. He just hoped she would manage to look older than sixteen. Maybe he could add it into their contract.

Deborah was staring at him. "Doesn't it bother you at all that I don't want to do this?"

"I can live with it," he assured her.

She muttered something he didn't catch.

"You're the one who started all this," he reminded her again.

"Yes, and I'm also the one who's volunteered to make it up to you in other ways!" she snapped. Then her eyes flickered and her cheeks reddened, and Cam-eron realized her thoughts were moving along the same lines his were. That surprised him, coming from someone so innocent. She emitted purity like some women did perfume.

"I could wash your car every week for a month," she offered hastily. "You know, that fancy foreign silver thing you love so much."

Wash his car? Cam flinched. He couldn't help it.

"Ooo-kay," she said. "You'd rather die than let me touch your car. Fine." Her tone was light, but a hint of hurt filled her beautiful blue eyes.

Cam sighed. Damn. He was going to have to tell her. He'd hoped to avoid it, although that was probably an unrealistic hope, anyway, since he would need her cooperation.

"Look, I need you to help me with a little problem I have." He wasn't used to fumbling for words like this, but the whole situation was damned awkward. "I've got a business associate whose eighteen-year-old daughter has decided I'm..." He searched for an appropriate expression, didn't find one, and started over. "I mean, for some reason, she finds me—" He stopped. This was hopeless.

Deborah smiled faintly. "She has a crush on you?"

"Yes, that's it." He hoped he didn't look as embarrassed as he felt. "Anyway, since her father's divorced and she usually goes to functions with him, it's a safe bet she'll be at the party." He grimaced. "Heather's very young, and she's had a rough time with her parents' divorce. The last thing I want to do is hurt her feelings. It'll be much easier all around if I'm otherwise attached." Attached to a *woman,* he wanted to emphasize. But this wasn't the time to point out that Deborah would have to mature herself for his party. He'd cover that later.

"I see," Deborah said slowly. She was looking at him strangely, as if something about him puzzled her. For a long moment she said nothing at all. Finally she asked, "How attached are we talking here? Moderately or intensely?"

Cam stifled a smile at her pink cheeks and the hint of wariness on her face. How would she react if he insisted they needed to appear intensely involved? The impulse to find out was almost overwhelming, but he ignored it the way he ignored all impulses. "Moderately would do, I'm sure." Cam examined the resigned expression that now appeared on her face. "You'll do it?"

Her sigh told him everything he needed to know.

Chapter Three

"So I agreed to do it," Deborah said later that afternoon as she sat on a stool in the large kitchen of
Sweetness and Light. From behind her came the con-
stant hum of conversation in the gourmet shop's small
café area. Scents of coffee and cinnamon rolls filled
the air.

Ann Medford dropped a spoonful of salmon
mousse into a pastry casing. "And you want me to
do the catering."

"Exactly."

"All right, I'll work you in. But only because it's
you." Her friend grinned. "And because I'm curious
as all get-out about this guy's house. From what I
hear, it's got a kitchen to die for."

"How did you hear that?" Deborah sampled a
spoonful of the salmon mousse. She was just making
conversation, of course. She couldn't care less about
Cameron Lyle's house.

"I heard it from Stella. You know, up at Rags to
Riches. One of her customers designed his kitchen,
and she said the whole house was beautiful." Ann
whirled away to check on the pans of cinnamon rolls
in the huge steel oven. She was only a few inches

over five feet, but energy pulsed from her almost visibly. She was back within seconds. "Stella also said that another of her customers dated him for months, but she was never invited to his house."

"Hmm." Deborah dipped another spoon into the mousse.

Ann nodded. "That's exactly what *I* said. He must be the private type. Hey, Deb, cool it with the mousse, would you? I'm going to have too many shells left over."

"No problem. I can fix that." Deborah reached for a puff pastry shell.

Ann swatted her hand away. "Didn't you eat lunch?" She pushed a strand of her short black hair back into her hair net.

"Sure." Deborah watched her deposit the tray of filled pastry shells on a rack. "If you call a peanut butter sandwich lunch."

"I don't, but you've probably been known to call it dinner, too."

"Only when I serve it with macaroni and cheese." Deborah chuckled. "You look like you're going to faint."

"Philistine," Ann muttered. She plunked a ball of dough down on her pastry board.

"Not at all. I know great food when I eat it. Like these hors d'oeuvre. We'll have to have some of these at the party." She could easily eat a dozen or so right now, but Ann was armed and the rolling pin was marble, so that was a bad idea.

"I wonder why the hunky Mr. Lyle asked you to be his hostess?" Ann mused.

"I already told you why," Deborah said. "I owe him."

"I know what you told me, but that seems like a weird reason to me." Her eyes narrowed. "I bet he has the hots for you."

Deborah laughed. Several customers at the counter looked over in their direction, so she lowered her voice. "Trust me, Cameron Lyle doesn't see me that way at all. He just needs a hostess and I'm handy." A pushover, too, apparently. One little tale of woe and he had her agreeing in no time flat. Her only excuse was that his apparent compassion for a teenager had caught her by surprise. Who'd have thought the guy was capable of that kind of empathy?

Of course, she hadn't ever pictured him apologizing to her for past rudeness, either. Another stunner.

"Oh, please." Ann sounded exasperated. "As if he couldn't come up with a party hostess on his own. From what we've both heard *and* seen, Indy's 'Most Eligible Bachelor' has women lining up."

Deborah grimaced. Money and good looks were apparently some women's major criteria. She herself, on the other hand, cared about things like personality. And even though his seemed to have improved today, it still left a lot to be desired. Which was why, even if he did make her heart beat a little faster and her palms tingle, she had nothing to worry about.

He was completely resistible.

"Maybe he's tired of female attention," Deborah suggested. "Maybe the fact that I'm not interested is a plus." After all, he certainly wasn't interested in her. Even though Cameron Lyle apparently didn't actually disapprove of her, it was clear he thought her an irritating and naïve creature. Those qualities made her a perfectly safe candidate to hostess his party. They also should have taken her out of the running for planning his party, but it was obvious he wasn't going to give her free rein, anyway, so he probably figured he was safe enough.

"Not interested, huh?" Ann gave her a searching look. "You know, Deb, I'm a little worried about you."

Deborah grinned. "Come off it, Ann."

"No, really, I'm serious. You're way too blasé about hostessing this guy's party. He's got every woman between sixteen and sixty panting after him, and you're not interested."

Ann pulled up a stool for herself and leaned in closer to Deborah. "I could understand it if Mark had broken your heart, but that's obviously not true. I mean, you moped around for all of two days, and then there you were, Ms. Sunshine again. Which I don't understand, either." Her deep gray eyes stared into Deborah's. "Are you okay? Come on, tell Auntie Ann."

In spite of her friend's light tones, her concern was obvious, and Deborah was touched. "I'm fine, Ann. Couldn't be better." Well, she could if she didn't have this hostessing nonsense hanging over her head, but that was a different issue, and she would deal with it.

"Really?" Ann looked dubious.

"Yes. As a matter of fact, when Mark broke off our engagement, I learned a couple of important things. One was that I'd gotten engaged to him mostly to please my mom. I was depressed for a day or so, but I didn't feel like I'd lost the love of my life. That wasn't the problem at all." She drew a breath. "What really got to me was that yet another man in my life had left me."

"Oh." Ann's voice was soft. "That makes sense. Your dad—"

"Yeah." Deborah swallowed. "There's no good age to have your father walk out on you, but it sure as heck was no fun at thirteen. And then there was Rick."

"Rick?" Her friend frowned. "You've never mentioned him."

"True. That's because I hadn't thought about him in years, until Mark broke our engagement. Anyway, Rick was my first serious boyfriend. He joined up to fight in the Gulf War and then stayed in the army. He found someone else and sent me a Dear Jane letter." She could smile about it now, but the teenage Deborah had been devastated.

Ann's lips tightened. "Jerk. What bad luck."

"That's one way of looking at it," Deborah agreed. "But I always knew Rick was sold on the armed forces, so if I'd thought about it, I could have predicted he'd leave. As for Mark..." She shook her head. "I realized it wasn't me, personally, he'd rejected. He just wasn't ready to get married. And neither was I, at least not to him."

Ann nodded. "There are much more exciting guys out there. You just have to look a little." She paused. "And when opportunity knocks, you have to take advantage of it."

Deborah eyed Ann's bright smile and knew exactly where her thoughts were heading. "Maybe. If it's the right opportunity."

"Exactly." Ann arranged the dough in several pie dishes. Then she looked up. "You have to admit Cameron Lyle is gorgeous. Plus, according to Stella, he's very generous with clothes for his lady friends.

You could enjoy his company without taking him seriously. He's probably a lot of fun.''

Fun. It wasn't the word Deborah would have used to describe him, even if she'd wanted to dwell on that particular word. Which she didn't. *Fun* reminded her of the gleam in Cameron's eyes as he asked her what kind they were having.

But she shouldn't be thinking about that, or about any of the various disturbing images that came to mind. She should be thinking only about getting through this party. Afterward, her contact level with him would be back to the usual hello. It would involve no fun at all.

And definitely no R-rated fun.

THE NEXT MORNING, Deborah took her paperwork down to Cameron. When Barb Metzen, his plump, middle-aged assistant, showed her into his office, he was sitting at his massive cherry desk. Today he wore a charcoal suit. Reading glasses perched on his nose. For some reason, they made him look even more attractive. Distinguished, in fact. His dark hair gleamed in the sunlight that slanted through the window.

He smiled at her, and Deborah felt an unwelcome little jolt hit her spine.

''I've got your proposal ready. And I need you to sign the contract.'' How annoying to find herself rushing into speech. She accepted a chair. ''After you look it over, of course.''

He ignored the papers. He was looking her over instead, his gaze traveling slowly from her ponytail to her bright floral sweatshirt to her red leggings and back up again. As usual, the intensity of his green eyes started a slow heat in her middle.

Deborah decided to go on the offensive. "So how come you don't have a hostess for this party?"

He raised a brow. "I do. You're not backing out, are you?"

"I meant from *before*," she told him. "I don't understand why you're having to come up with someone right now, at the eleventh hour." She should have thought of that right away. She probably would have, too, if she hadn't been so dismayed and generally shaken by his request.

"I did have a hostess," Cameron admitted. "She canceled." He took a few sips from the huge coffee mug on his desk. Then he twirled a pencil, watching it closely. He looked more uncomfortable than she'd ever seen him.

Sudden suspicion hit her. "You mean she ditched you?"

Cameron looked up but said nothing. His gaze wasn't encouraging.

Deborah fought a smile. "She did, didn't she?" It wasn't nice to bait him, but this was too good not to follow up. Besides, what about all the grief Mr. High-and-Mighty had given her? Was still giving her, for that matter?

"Touché." He sent her a wry nod. "Yes, you could say she ditched me."

"Why?"

He looked surprised by her question, and at first she thought he was going to ignore it. Then he shrugged. "I guess she figured out I meant what I said, and she wasn't going to get what she wanted."

"Which was…?" None of this was any of her business, of course, but his opinion of her was already somewhere between iffy and unfavorable, so she might as well satisfy her curiosity.

"Marriage," Cameron said. Then he cleared his throat and glanced down at the papers she'd brought, as if he'd only just seen them. In cats, that kind of look indicated embarrassment. With this man, who knew?

"So in fact you're the one who broke up with her."

He frowned but didn't answer.

"She's the redhead?" Deborah asked before she could stop herself.

He stared at her.

Her cheeks felt suddenly warm. "I think I saw you with a redhead one time," she mumbled. Why couldn't she learn to keep a lid on it?

"I see. No, that was somebody before her." A hint of red crept into his tanned cheeks.

Deborah nodded. Even if she hadn't been fully aware of his reputation, she wouldn't have needed to ask if he'd been the one to break off that relationship and if so, why. His expression told the whole story. It told her one other thing, loud and clear: This man was a menace to women.

Deborah gave him a long, measuring look. "I get it. You're one of those."

"One of those what?" He frowned again, more vigorously this time. His dark brows almost met over the bridge of his nose. He looked more like the man she'd watched from a safe distance, the man who frowned at the least little thing she said or did.

Too bad, because yesterday he'd been an actual human being, and aside from dumping women right and left, he'd seemed almost likeable.

"You know, if you're not careful, all that frowning

is going to give you deep wrinkles," Deborah warned. She had no idea if he was the type to worry about wrinkles, but in any case, the look on his face was priceless.

"You should smile more," she told him. "Frowning isn't good for you, but smiling is. Did you know that? Smiling makes you feel happier, which lowers your stress level and keeps your heart healthier. In fact—"

"What am I one of?" he demanded again, his face a strange mixture of affront, curiosity and reluctance, as if he was asking the question against his better judgment.

Deborah shrugged. "Well, I don't know this for sure, of course. It's just a guess. But it seems to me like you're one of those afraid-to-make-a-commitment guys." Thanks to Mark, she could now see one coming a mile away.

His frown darkened. "I am not. What a load of nonsense."

She eyed him. "You know, you sound really stressed. I bet that's not the first mug of coffee you've had today, is it?"

His expression answered her.

"That mug must hold three cups, at least. Caffeine is another stress inducer."

He folded his arms over his chest. "Is that right?"

"Absolutely. You really should consider cutting back."

"Or maybe throwing you out of my office, which would also relieve my stress level," he pointed out.

She laughed. "Really? Okay, fair enough. It was rude of me to come in here and point out your commitment problems."

He shrugged. "Actually, it doesn't matter. Your analysis is incorrect, anyway."

"Fine," she said, and waved a hand with airy unconcern. "I'm sure you're right. You're not commitment phobic. Any year now you'll take the plunge and after all, you're only, what, thirty-five?"

He ignored the question. "And what makes you an expert on all this female psychobabble stuff?"

Deborah shrugged. She could tell him she'd majored in psychology, which might make him sit up and pay attention. But since no amount of creative math could turn foreign languages plus education into psychology, she contented herself with giving him a Mona Lisa smile. "I wasn't born yesterday."

"Maybe not yesterday, but pretty damned close," he muttered.

Her eyes narrowed. "What's that supposed to mean?"

"It means you're too young to know much about men or relationships."

Deborah raised her brows at him in imitation of his own habit. "I'm twenty-seven, and that's a very pompous thing to say." Why was she surprised?

"Twenty-seven?" Shock showed in the bottle-green eyes.

"Yes. How old are you?" Would he tell her? Not that she really cared how old he was, of course. Cameron Lyle didn't interest her. But she deserved to know his age since he knew hers. It was the principle of the thing.

"Thirty-one," he said. "Are you sure you're twenty-seven?" He looked her over, his gaze lingering on her face.

No prizes for guessing what he saw. Blue eyes,

slightly rounded pink cheeks and wisps of blond hair
escaping from her ponytail. Nothing special. Definitely not a sophisticated picture, either. She was getting tired of comments about not looking her age.

"You look barely out of college," he added, still
looking stunned.

Several pithy retorts came to mind, but with great
effort Deborah ignored them all. "We were talking
about you," she reminded him.

"Maybe we were, but we're not anymore. You
know absolutely nothing about the situation." Cameron sent her a steely-eyed glance that said she wasn't
getting any more information out of him. "You're
just feeling hostile toward men right now, and you're
taking it out on me."

"I'm not feeling hostile." Relieved was the word.
It was scary how close she'd come to marrying Mark.

Cameron raised a brow. "Yes, you are. You're also
highly annoyed that you're stuck going to my party."

Deborah pulled a face. That part she couldn't deny.

He chuckled. "Cheer up. I'll take you shopping
and we'll find you a dress that will make the whole
ordeal bearable for you."

She frowned. "Shopping?" She shouldn't be so
horrified. No doubt there were many things that
would be more awful than a shopping trip with this
man.

Major surgery and death were the first two that
came to mind.

Any shopping she and Cameron Lyle did together
would entail nonstop arguments. If she paid any attention to his opinions, she'd wind up with the
world's most tasteful and most boring dress, one that

would put her into a coma as soon as she saw herself in the mirror.

"Yes, shopping," he said. "I know a good boutique just up the street."

Rags to Riches. Stella's shop. Deborah winced. The gossips would have a field day. It didn't bear thinking about.

"No shopping," she said. "I don't need a dress, and even if I did, I certainly wouldn't need you to help me pick it out." Did he want to make sure she matched the napkins?

"I'm sure you wouldn't. And I guess I could reimburse you later, but using my credit card seems easier."

He planned to pay? Shock kept her silent for several seconds, but then she swallowed the anger that rose in her throat. Why was she surprised he was the type who liked throwing his money around?

"You're not paying for my dress." Deborah said it slowly and succinctly, so there would be no ambiguity.

He looked surprised. "Why not? You're hostessing my party for me. Consider this one of the job's perks. I assure you, I can easily afford it."

"That's not the point," she said tightly. How many different ways could this man find to insult her? No wonder her sense of humor took a hike every time he opened his mouth.

She met his gaze and Deborah could see that he honestly had no idea he was insulting her. *Men!* She could see it right now. There she'd be, parading in front of him in evening dresses, each more skimpy than the last. Watching his gaze move slowly over her. Standing next to him while he paid for one of them. Just like one of his interchangeable girlfriends.

Every nerve in her body twitched. *"No."*

Cameron's formidable jaw set. "Anybody ever tell you how stubborn you are?"

"All the time, when I was a teenager."

You're so stubborn, Deborah. She could still hear her father's voice, filled with exasperation.

And hear herself, slamming her bedroom door.

"Most women would jump at the chance to buy a new dress," Cameron pointed out.

"I'm not most women." And she was definitely not *his* woman. Buying her a dress would probably mean nothing to Cameron, but Deborah knew how she would feel.

Bought. Owned.

"Don't forget, you'll need to look older than Heather," he pointed out. "I take it you have a suitable dress?" He looked doubtful, leaving her to wonder how he thought she'd define the word *suitable.*

Deborah suspected she knew the answer to that question. Cameron imagined her to be an artsy, naïve type who thought dangly earrings were the height of sophistication. The rise of his brows and the slow progress of his gaze over her sweatshirt and leggings confirmed her suspicions. He probably figured she'd show up in tiered ruffles looking like his date for the prom.

Deborah sent him a bland smile. "Don't worry. I'll keep my ruffled pink-and-orange floral in the closet."

The look on his face made her smile all the way back to her apartment.

Chapter Four

Everything Cam knew about Deborah Clark made one fact stunningly clear.

Unengaged or not, she was still off-limits to him.

Cam stood outside her apartment door and took in her well-scrubbed, fresh girl-next-door look. This girl—*woman*—did not have much experience with men.

For once she wasn't wearing her usual uniform of leggings paired with a long, baggy and very bright top. Today she wore a black suit that contrasted well with her golden hair. Even though it followed her curves faithfully, the suit itself was conservative enough. Combined as it was with pumps and tasteful hoop earrings, it would be at home in any of the city's office buildings.

Except for the fuchsia blouse she wore with it. Startling in color and design, the blouse was pure Deborah, a splash of individuality in the midst of conformity.

Her blouse made him want to smile, and so did her hair. She wore her usual ponytail, except that today she'd put one of those scrunched-up fabric things around it. But if she thought a black hair accessory made for a more sophisticated look, he had news for her, because in spite of her business gear, Deborah still looked about sixteen. Cute—*very cute*...

"Hi," Cam said after a long pause.

Her gaze met his and he thought he saw a small flicker of awareness in the bright blue depths, but he couldn't tell, because she gave him only a brief glance before striding over to her desk and rummaging through it. "I'll be right with you. I'm running a little late this morning." Her voice had a brisk, electric quality to it, as if she was primed and ready for action.

"I guess you have somewhere else you need to be," he observed in the most neutral tones he could come up with. He was stating the obvious, of course, since he had never seen her in a suit before.

"Only at lunchtime. I've still got an hour." Deborah stopped rummaging through her desk and took a folder out of the filing cabinet in the corner of her living room. Her movements were quick and decisive.

Cam heard a faint sound and turned his head toward it. In stark contrast to her owner's energized appearance, Libby lay stretched out on the sofa, fast asleep. The cat's white belly rose and fell in a slow, gentle rhythm.

Cam's gaze returned to Deborah. Everything about her seemed sharper, more focused. She crackled with electricity.

Whatever this lunch was about, it meant a lot to her.

What could be so important to Deborah Clark, who seemed to take nothing seriously? He had no idea. But judging from her business dress, it had something to do with work.

Work. The reason he was here.

"Why don't you show me what you have so far?" Cam kept his gaze away from her gracefully crossed legs.

The party was still nearly two weeks away, which allowed him plenty of time to troubleshoot. Also, it was not a crucial business function, so there was a margin for error. Just as long as error didn't turn into disaster. Making sure that didn't happen was, of course, why he was here.

Deborah handed him a folder. "I still think you should consider a more interesting décor than a few floral arrangements, but if you're sure that's all you want...."

"I'm sure." Cam flipped through the folder and felt his amazement grow with every page. He suppressed a whistle.

She'd done a hell of a lot in a short time period. She'd done it well, too, judging by the very organized looking checklists, detailed vendor information and the variety of menu suggestions she included. It was all there, in what seemed to him the minutest of details.

Her chuckle made him look up. Cam found her amused eyes on him, and he realized his surprise must be obvious. To cover his discomfort, he lifted a brow in polite inquiry.

"Go ahead and admit it. You're floored I can make lists. I assure you, it's a common reaction. Especially from people who don't know me very well." Her smile was gentle but pointed, tinged faintly with challenge.

Cam got the message. And she had a point. He didn't know her well. In fact, he was beginning to suspect he didn't know her at all. The thought made him uneasy.

"You don't seem like a list maker," he said.

"I'm not, in private life. But details are crucial in my line of work, because people feel strongly about special occasions. When you commit to planning someone's party, you've got to get it right the first time. You owe your client the best event you can possibly produce." Deborah didn't look amused anymore.

Cam stared at her. She looked more intense than he'd ever seen her. And her voice sounded unfamiliar. He heard enthusiasm and something else he couldn't identify.

"What many people don't understand," she continued, "is that details make all the difference in the world. They can transform an ordinary event into a truly spectacular one. And when you have the chance to create something memorable, you have to run with it, because you don't get second chances in event planning."

She leaned toward him. "It's not like selling clothes or coffee mugs, which can be exchanged if the customer isn't satisfied. Events are totally different. Whatever happens, you've got to make them right, because if they go wrong, you can't just tell clients and their guests to come back the following night."

Cam stared at her. *Passion.* That was it. That was what he heard in her voice.

"I guess not," he murmured. He'd never thought of it that way before. He'd also never imagined Deborah could be this intense about any topic, especially a work-related one. The laid-back, free-spirited attitude she usually projected hadn't prepared him for this kind of emotion.

Nothing had prepared him for his own reaction to it, either. He found himself wondering what it would be like if all her intensity were focused on him instead of work.

Deborah cleared her throat. "Sorry. I get a little carried away sometimes." She looked away, which was fine with Cam since it gave him more opportunity to study her.

It was strange the way her intensity had given her face a more mature cast. For a moment there, she'd looked fully adult. Deborah Clark was more interesting than he could have guessed. Cam watched her face as she wrote something on a tablet from her desk. She looked uncomfortable, as if she'd said too much. Which wasn't true. What she'd said didn't matter nearly as much as the way she'd said it. Now *that* was interesting.

"Anything else you'd like to discuss?" she asked.

Plenty. But he knew she was talking about his party. "It looks like I can safely leave it all to you," he said, and found that he meant it. Her job might be the only thing she took seriously, but he couldn't doubt her dedication to her work.

"Good," she said, and waited.

It didn't take much to figure out she was waiting for him to leave. Cam got up. In the lengthening silence, he searched for something else to say. The plain, bald truth was that he didn't want to go yet. He wanted to hear her talk some more about her work. He wanted to see that peculiar intensity light up her eyes again. He wanted to hear more passion in her voice.

But he shouldn't be thinking about any of that. Just because she turned out to be seriously, *intensely,* interested in her work, there was no reason to forget one undeniable fact.

Deborah Clark was an innocent and therefore off-limits to him. Period. End of story.

So he should head on out of here pronto. He should send Barb to lunch, grab a sandwich and a big mug of coffee for himself and get some of that ungodly mound of paperwork cleared off his desk.

"Who are you having lunch with?" he asked instead.

In the beat of silence that followed, Cam stifled a wince. How had that come out of his mouth? He never blurted out things. And he never asked nosy questions. That was Deborah's province. She was the one who grilled people about their love lives, nailing them to the wall and demanding to know if they'd been ditched. Were her habits rubbing off on him?

Perish the thought.

He wasn't worried about making her uncomfortable. After all, she'd gotten some definite mileage the other day out of his own embarrassment. And at least he wasn't pronouncing her commitment-phobic into the bargain. In fact, compared to her grilling, his small question was downright genteel.

No, he didn't mind embarrassing her a little. Girl or woman, Deborah could take care of herself. But he minded very much knowing that he'd lost control enough to ask a question he'd already decided he wasn't going to ask. He also minded her knowing about his curiosity.

Deborah was looking at him in almost comical surprise, as if she was just as floored as he was by his question.

"A client," she said after a moment.

"A client?" His head felt a little strange. Must be the last of the indiscretion-related shock waves reverberating in his brain.

"Well, *maybe* a client," Deborah amended. "He's the owner of a local clothing chain, and he's looking for someone to plan shareholders' meetings." She said it casually, but her eyes glowed with suppressed excitement. Twin dots of pink stained her cheeks. She looked cute again, which was a relief.

"This could be a big deal for your company, then," Cam noted, ignoring the small voice inside him that said she hadn't looked cute a few minutes ago. She'd looked vibrant and beautiful.

Passionate.

"It could, yes," she agreed.

"Congratulations."

Deborah shook her head. "I haven't gotten the contract yet." But she was smiling, and Cam had the feeling she expected to get it. And why shouldn't she? As far as he could tell, she did good work. She probably had a perfectly good business head on her shoulders.

Cam watched her cross to the sofa and pick up her coat and purse. That was when he noticed that Libby was still stretched out in the same position she'd been in when he arrived.

"Your cat's not exactly energetic, is she?" he observed.

Deborah surveyed her pet with a small, indulgent smile. "No."

"Isn't it time for her morning walk?" It was eleven

o'clock, just about the time the cat had shown up in his office. That day seemed a lot longer ago than only five weeks.

She looked puzzled. "What morning walk?"

"I thought she went out every morning," Cam said.

Deborah shook her head. "No. Libby doesn't venture out much. In fact, the day you found her, she'd escaped while I was in the shower, and I had no idea she'd gotten out."

That explained a lot. It explained not only Deborah's surprise when he'd handed over the cat, but also the little details he'd noticed at the time, like her damp, tousled hair and her glowing skin.

Little details he'd tried to forget.

"Cats aren't like dogs," Deborah pointed out. "You don't walk them every morning." Once more she looked amused.

"I don't know much about cats," Cam said. "We always had dogs when I was growing up."

"But you don't now." She still looked disappointed about his dogless state, and even knowing her disappointment was only that she was stuck hostessing his party instead of walking his dog, Cam found himself taking it personally.

"That's right. Now I have fish," he told her with a firm cheerfulness.

Her brows shot up. *"Fish?"*

Cam frowned.

"Sorry," Deborah muttered. "You just don't look like a fish person."

He stared at her.

"I'm sure you're wondering what a fish person looks like," she continued. "And I'd have to say I have no idea, but I pictured you with a very large dog.''

"My fish are the tropical kind,'' he told her. "I like to watch them, especially when I'm trying to figure out a business problem. They're soothing.'' He grinned. "You still look doubtful. Don't you like fish?''

She shrugged. "They're not furry, which is a major pet criterion for me. Also, you can't train them.''

"You can't train cats, either,'' Cam felt obliged to point out.

"Of course you can.'' As she provided him with examples it became clear that he'd hit on a powerful topic. She looked as if she'd completely forgotten about her business lunch. "You just have to make a few allowances for personality quirks,'' she finished.

"Hmm. I know what you mean,'' he said after a moment. "One of my fish is like that. Very quirky.''

"Really?'' She looked even more doubtful than before, and a little suspicious, too, as if she thought he might be putting her on.

Cam nodded. "Herbie. What a grump.''

She blinked. "Did you name all your fish?'' Her tone sounded carefully neutral.

"No. He's the only one who has much personality, to tell you the truth. He's almost the smallest one in the tank, but he's aggressive. He chases everyone else around.'' Cam watched her grin. Cute was a safer look for her than the passionate expression she'd worn a few minutes ago. A few thoughts about her cuteness were not going to get either of them in trouble.

"Shouldn't you be going to your lunch?'' he asked.

Deborah shot a look at her watch. "Yes, I should.

I've got just enough time to get there. Anyway, I guess I'll meet your fish before too long," she added, "because I'll need to see your house—the kitchen, the party site, et cetera—as soon as possible so I can plan the setup."

"Fine." For some reason he was actually looking forward to showing her around. "How about ten on Saturday morning?"

"I'll be there."

Cam smiled in satisfaction.

DEBORAH PULLED UP outside Cameron's house and gazed at it for a while. Her surprise that he lived outside of the city instead of in a posh neighborhood was nothing compared to the shock his house gave her.

It was large but not ostentatiously so. She'd imagined a huge modern monstrosity with pillars, intricate landscaping and a pool, but it wasn't like that. In fact, Cameron's house wasn't at all what she'd expected from a man as wealthy as he was, a man who made such a big splash in Indianapolis society.

It was a normal house. Understated, even. The two-story structure had wood on top and limestone on the bottom. Painted a green that matched the trees and bushes surrounding it, the house looked natural, as if it belonged there in the woods.

As Deborah got out of the car, she caught a movement from behind the big picture window, and then the front door opened and Cameron came down the walk. He looked relaxed in tan corduroys and a cream polo shirt.

As always, up close he was even bigger than she remembered, one of few men whose height forced her to tilt her head up. At five ten, Deborah wasn't used to feeling small and vulnerable. She didn't like it, either.

Maybe she should wear business suits all the time around this man. Having armor had certainly helped on Wednesday. Even though the intensity of his gaze had made her as uncomfortable as it always did, the knowledge that she looked pulled together had steadied her. For the first time since she'd met Cameron Lyle, her tongue hadn't run away with her. Well, except for her little lecture on event planning, but she could never control herself on that topic, no matter who she was talking to, so that didn't count.

"Nice place," Deborah told him. Her voice sounded too hearty, but at least she wasn't babbling. She'd been to lots of clients' houses, but this was the first time she'd planned an event for someone she was attracted to. Add that fact to the unfortunate truth that she had never in her life been this attracted to any man, and you had a recipe for possible disaster.

Getting this party over with would be a huge relief.

Meanwhile, planning it gave her something to think about besides the depressing news she'd received yesterday.

"Thanks. Come on in." Cameron guided her inside, one hand between her shoulder blades, and she was way too aware of the warmth of his hand on her back. Deborah swallowed, but then the view caught her attention and she gasped.

She was looking at woods again, because the entire far wall was glass. The house sat on a hill, so through the glass she saw a large deck, and beyond it, sloping masses of evergreens. Sunlight reflected off the thin layer of snow remaining on the ground, and bright red cardinals were busy at the birdfeeders on the deck. The tranquil scene was straight from a Christmas card.

"It's beautiful," Deborah said finally.

"You like it?" Cameron looked pleased by her reaction. His smile lightened his features and made him even more dangerously attractive. Unlike some of the smiles he'd given her in the past, this one reached his eyes. As always, their vivid green gave her a small shock of pleasure.

"Yes, I do." She moved away from the window. Away from him.

Business. That was what she was here for.

"You should have told me you have an incredible view." Deborah heard the accusation in her voice, but she couldn't suppress it.

Cameron raised a brow. "Why?"

"Because with built-in décor like this, we could do something really spectacular." The mere thought of the ho-hum floral arrangements they'd settled on made her want to gnash her teeth. What a wasted opportunity.

Something of what she felt must have shown on her face, because he was watching her intently. "Such as...?"

"Such as a winter scene that incorporates the view from your glass wall." The more she thought about it, the more excited Deborah got. "A park, for example. A beautiful, snowy park."

"A snowy park?" Cameron looked around his living room, skepticism clearly written on his face. That was understandable, since his living room featured hardwood floors and comfortable, overstuffed furniture in warm shades of brown, apricot and beige.

Nothing about the room suggested a park in the middle of winter.

But it would when she was finished with it.

"Trust me, it can be done. We'll have to hustle, since we've only got ten days left, but fortunately, all we're changing is the décor. And I have the perfect supplier."

He shook his head. "No. We can't change the décor."

Deborah met his gaze squarely. "You could have a truly fantastic, memorable event here, one your guests will talk about for years."

He watched her with unreadable eyes. "What if I prefer a sensible, traditional event?"

She took a deep breath. There was no point in getting bent out of shape. This man was, after all, the client. He had to be comfortable with the event design.

Deborah inclined her head. "If you really want something traditional, that's what we'll go with."

Cameron's sudden, mischievous grin took her by surprise. "And so you're giving up, just like that?"

"You're the client," she reminded him, stifling a surge of irritation. The dratted man was playing with her. He probably had no idea how important this party was to her. And even if he did, would that change anything? If Cameron realized this was the first business function she'd ever planned, would it matter to a man as wealthy as he was?

Deborah wouldn't want to bet on it.

"How soon could you get a revised proposal to me?" he asked.

She fought the urge to shout.

"By the end of the weekend," Deborah assured him.

"Okay, we'll see what you can do. Meanwhile, I'll show you the rest of the ground floor, starting with the kitchen. What can I get you to drink?"

Just like that, he turned into the perfect host. She was never going to understand this man. Good thing she didn't have to. All she had to do was produce the best party he—or his guests—had ever attended.

Juice glass in hand, Deborah followed Cameron around the house, which was fully as beautiful as she'd anticipated, although in a different way. It was—she searched for the word—*warm*. Sophisticated but charming.

She'd expected a museum and instead found a home. The fact that Cameron Lyle had a lot of money was obvious only in the beautiful craftsmanship of his house and the generous number and size of rooms. His furnishings, while attractive, were simple and masculine, as if he'd picked them out himself instead of hiring a decorator. All in all, very little about his house fit the image she had of Cameron Lyle.

Maybe she'd misjudged him as completely as she had Clint Barry, the man she'd fully expected to become her client.

Deborah shoved that depressing thought away.

After touring the downstairs, they ended up back in his living room. Deborah found her gaze drawn to the aquarium next to the stone fireplace.

"So here are your fish." She looked into the tank of brightly colored, active creatures. "And there's Herbie."

"Hard to spot, isn't he?" Cameron said dryly.

"I see what you mean about his aggression." The

tiny blue fish swam straight into the path of several yellow angelfish, causing them to dart off, with Herbie in hot pursuit.

"I'm going to have to do something about him," Cameron said. "But not today. Ready to see the upstairs?" He smiled at her.

Deborah blinked. *Upstairs?* She couldn't. She simply couldn't go see bedrooms with this man.

"Oh, I don't need to look at that," she said in as breezy a voice as possible. "It's not part of the event site, is it?" The chirpiness of her voice made her want to wince.

"That's true." He looked oddly disappointed, though, which made no sense. Wasn't this the man who didn't even invite his girlfriends to his home? Why was he being the perfect host this morning, plying her with orange juice and looking ready to hang out with her indefinitely?

The answer, in the end, was obvious.

She was not his girlfriend. In his eyes, she wasn't even an eligible woman. Because Cameron didn't see her as a woman. He knew exactly how old she was, but he still thought of her as a girl, and Deborah knew why.

She looked too young and way too unsophisticated.

"Hey, I never asked how your business lunch went," Cameron said. "You got the contract?"

"No," Deborah told him. "No, I didn't." Figuring out why hadn't been tough, either. In both of their previous phone conversations, Clint Barry had been enthusiastic and impressed with the proposal she'd sent him.

Then he'd taken one look at her and decided she was too wet behind the ears to handle the job.

The surprise on his face when he'd seen her, as well as the faintly patronizing tinge to his half of their lunchtime conversation made his thinking crystal clear.

Deborah's face still burned when she thought about that lunch meeting.

So she'd better not think about it. Time to move on.

"I'm sorry," Cameron was saying.

Deborah shrugged. "You win some, you lose some." It wasn't the way she felt, and she knew he knew it. But Deborah also knew that this was the last contract she would lose because of an unsophisticated image. This was the last time a handsome man—or any man—would dismiss her as naïve and innocent.

It was time to change her image.

Chapter Five

Where was Deborah?

Cam looked at his watch. Almost a quarter to seven. Only forty-five minutes before the first guests showed up.

The caterer and her team were installed in his kitchen, from which wafted mouthwatering aromas of beef, wine sauce and rich buttery pastry. The bartender had set up in one corner of the dining room. Melodious strains that sounded like Bach came from the study, where the musicians were warming up. In fact, all key personnel were here, with one notable exception.

Deborah.

She'd been here this morning, directing traffic in a take-charge voice he'd never heard before. It was a voice that commanded attention, and it sure as hell had gotten his, because it was a far cry from the light, amused voice he'd always heard from Deborah before.

Always, with one exception. That day in her home office, as she'd discussed her work, he'd heard enough passion in Deborah's voice to make him imagine things he shouldn't be imagining. Things like rumpled sheets, blond hair across his pillow and a voice just like that one calling his name.

Cam frowned. This was ridiculous, not to say inconvenient. The darned girl—no, *woman*—had hijacked his thoughts. Not to mention his house. Cam barely recognized the place.

He now had a frozen winter park in his living room. He wouldn't have believed it possible—hell, he *hadn't* believed it possible—but there it was. Bare birch trees stood everywhere, stark and white. Large stone urns overflowed with "snow" and narcissus. A fountain filled with ice carvings created the look of water frozen in mid-cascade. Encircling the fountain was still more narcissus. Grouped around the wood parquet dance floor, six tables set with steel blue linens and sparkling crystal added to the icy look. So did skillful blue-and-white lighting.

The outdoor scene was no less spectacular. Powerful spotlights made the evergreens beyond his deck visible through the glass wall of his living room. The park theme continued on the deck, with several wrought iron benches and old-fashioned lampposts providing additional atmosphere. Even the weather had cooperated, producing a light dusting of white for the trees.

It was a spectacular winter scene, so much more interesting than his original plan of a simple burgundy and silver theme for his party. Furthermore, this winter park was a natural extension of the wooded scene already present outside the huge glass wall of his living room.

It was a brilliant idea. Deborah had been right on target.

But where the hell *was* she?

Cam saw her then and promptly lost his train of thought.

Good God.

Deborah stood a dozen yards away from him in a green dress that shot his blood pressure through the roof. The elegant, halter-style gown showed off her long, graceful neck. The front of the dress hugged her breasts, the square neckline showing a hint of cleavage. The dress nipped sharply in at the waist before falling in a full, flowing skirt to the floor.

Cam's gaze returned to her rounded breasts, lingering there until, with an effort, he dragged it away. As he watched her, Deborah said a few more words to the caterer before moving in Cam's direction.

The closer she got, the more amazing she looked. Deborah was attractive without makeup. With it, she was nothing short of gorgeous. Her eyes were giant pools of blue ringed with thick, dark lashes. A subtle shadowing enhanced her elegant cheekbones. Glossy red made her already full lips look incredibly kissable. She'd piled her blond hair on top of her head in a sophisticated style. The emerald green color of the dress made her eyes and hair look brighter, her skin creamier.

Cam took a slow, careful breath. Deborah looked incredible. She looked like a walking male fantasy. She looked like...

Trouble. That's what she looked like. Big trouble.

Cam swallowed. His inconvenient but manageable attraction to this woman had just ballooned into a highly inconvenient and damned near uncontrollable desire. He had to get a grip. He had to remember that this woman was not his type. She might look like his type tonight—hell, talk about an understatement—but that didn't mean anything. He and Deborah Clark still had nothing in common.

And she still had extremely innocent eyes.

His last thought finally broke the spell he'd been under. As Deborah reached his side, Cam cleared his throat. "You're late. Where have you been?" His voice sounded rusty, but at least it was working. And at least he wasn't staring at her like an idiot anymore.

For a split second, he saw annoyance and something else that looked like hurt in Deborah's eyes, but then she gave him one of her supernaturally calm, patient looks. "I've been right here, taking care of last-minute details. Don't worry, everything's going to be fine." Her soothing smile had the opposite effect. He wanted to kiss it right off her face. He wanted to do other things, too. Things he should not be thinking about, at least not in connection with this woman.

"How do you like the finished décor?" Deborah waved a hand to indicate his frozen-over living room.

Cam followed her gesture and struggled to concentrate. "It's stunning. You've done a terrific job." It was nothing less than the truth, even though he was late in saying it. A sincere compliment on her work should have been the first thing out of his mouth, and instead he'd given her criticism. He knew why, too, and the knowledge unsettled him even more.

"Thanks." Deborah accepted his compliment calmly, but as she surveyed his living room, there was nothing calm about her expression. Cam watched her eyes light up. The enthusiasm she brought to her work, and to life in general, was incredibly attractive. There was nothing blasé about Deborah, none of the world-weariness that passed for sophistication in so many of the people he knew.

Especially the women he dated.

Cam frowned. He wasn't going to think about his boring social life right now. He wasn't going to think about how there wasn't a single woman in his social circle who he wanted to spend time with, never mind take to the various events he'd be attending over the next few months.

Most of all, he wasn't going to think about his surprise—and his dismay—at the increased temptation Deborah Clark had just presented him with.

THEY HAD ALMOST finished dinner. Deborah took a quick, gratified glance at the guests' mostly empty plates. The butternut squash soup and the beef in pastry were both hits, the perfect hot food to accompany a wintry setting. Ann and her team had pulled out all the stops, and the guests were clearly appreciative.

They loved the décor, too. That much was clear from every murmur and exclamation. In fact, the whole party was going so well that Deborah should have been over the moon.

She would be, too, if the host weren't so distracting that concentration on anything else was difficult. And if she weren't stuck playing hostess, a role that felt way too intimate. This was much worse than she had bargained for.

Cameron looked too good in formal black and white. Furthermore, he was the ideal host, smiling and attentive. In fact, he was more charming than Deborah had ever seen him before. If this was his usual social persona, no wonder women fell for him by the dozen.

His smiles made her pulse quicken. And when he touched her… She wiped her palms on her napkin. Even the most casual touch of his strong, warm fingers sent tiny shivers through her. Every time he leaned toward her to whisper a guest's name in her ear, Deborah felt her nerves stretch a little tighter. Her brain was working overtime tonight reminding her that she and this man were polar opposites in every way that counted.

And that he specialized in dumping women.

The last thought should have brought her galloping hormones to an instant, screeching halt. The fact that it didn't both alarmed and annoyed her. To make matters worse, the attraction she felt was obviously one-sided. Beneath Cameron's charm, she detected only a strange kind of caution. There was no hint he'd noticed anything different about her. As far as he was concerned, she could be wearing her usual leggings and sweatshirt. She could be wearing pink-and-orange ruffles, for heaven's sake.

Deborah took the last sip of her wine. It was a good thing her decision to change her image was purely business related. She didn't care what Cameron thought. She was here solely to hostess his party and rescue him from the amorous clutches of an eighteen-year-old.

Deborah might have suspected Cameron of making up the entire problem with Heather if it weren't for the lingering, wistful look the young girl had given him and her narrow-eyed, assessing stare at Deborah.

But before long Heather had turned her attention to the attractive young man Cameron introduced her to. It was all smoothly handled and seemingly casual. Except that Deborah had felt the tension in Cameron's hand as it rested lightly on her shoulder. She'd felt that tension release as they watched Heather laugh at a teasing remark her admirer made. Naturally, his concern for a teenager's feelings made Deborah like him more, which was a drag, since she didn't *want* to like Cameron any more than she did.

And now here she sat, trying to ignore the veiled curiosity in the shrewd brown eyes of Hazel Myers, a longtime client of Cameron's. The older woman's curiosity echoed the interest Deborah had seen on other faces. After all, Indianapolis' "Most Eligible Bachelor" was a man who drew public interest. She could hardly expect to show up out of obscurity as his hostess and escape notice.

She would simply have to make the best of it.

Only seconds after Hazel Myers excused herself, Deborah felt the warmth of Cameron's hand on her bare arm, making her skin tingle all the way from her wrist to her shoulder.

"It's time to dance," he said. "Together. You and me," he added in obvious response to her blank look.

Dance? With Cameron Lyle? When a few touches on her arm already had her about to jump out of her skin?

No. She'd made it through dinner, but why press her luck? Spending a whole dance with this man, his sinfully attractive body pressed next to hers, was a bad plan. Probably an invitation to disaster.

"That's not a good idea," Deborah said, speaking quietly enough that she hoped no one could overhear.

He looked amused. "Of course it is. Besides, it's traditional. The host and hostess start the dancing."

"Well, I can't dance." That announcement was more desperate than accurate, but she couldn't help it. Plus, for all she knew, it might be true tonight. Something about Cameron made her feel like she was hanging out over a cliff. Having his arms around her might send her right over the edge.

"I think you should ask someone else." She winced at how gauche that sounded. "I mean, I know I'm paying off a debt tonight, but I'm sure that as host and hostess, we can think of other things to do besides dancing. I'm also sure there are lots of women here who'd love to dance with you. Besides, the whole point of the evening is to have fun, and what fun would you have with a partner who has two left feet? Worse than that, really. My last partner ended up in a foot cast, and I'm sure that's not a risk you want to take." Deborah stopped for breath.

Cameron shrugged. "So you can't dance. You can talk, can't you?" He gave a sudden, explosive laugh. "My God, yes. You sure as hell can talk." His laughter changed his whole face, softening it and filling it with warmth. His eyes twinkled down at her.

Deborah's heartbeat picked up speed. But even though she couldn't help responding to the look in his eyes, chagrin filled her. So much for her new image. If she had to argue with the man, couldn't she at least do it with style? Good grief. Why didn't she just throw a two-year-old tantrum while she was at it?

She gathered the shreds of her dignity. "Okay, okay. I know sometimes I talk too much." The thing was, it only happened around him. How ridiculous. It wasn't as if she'd never talked to an attractive man before.

Still, she'd never torn the clothes off one. And she wanted to keep it that way.

"Don't worry about it. You can talk all you want while we shuffle around on the dance floor." He was still smiling. "As a matter of interest, what other activities were you suggesting we engage in?" He gave her a slow perusal with eyes that held a teasing glint.

Deborah watched the green of his eyes deepen and, for a few seconds, confusion took hold of her. Then his meaning sank in and she stared at him in shock.

Cameron Lyle was flirting with her.

Her pulse hammered so hard she was afraid he could hear it even over the music. And judging by how hot her face felt, it had gone several shades pinker. Darn it. Why read anything into his gentle flirtation? Cameron was simply having a good time at his party.

Repeat and repeat again: This man is not interested in you. And you are definitely not interested in him.

Exactly.

CAM PULLED Deborah a little closer to avoid collision with another couple. Now that he'd finally persuaded her she should dance with him, it wouldn't do to have her wiped out in the first dance. Or to step on her feet himself, which was inevitable if he didn't stop thinking about how soft and smooth her skin was under his hands, how good her hair smelled and how close her lips were to his.

"How long have you been an event planner?" he asked.

"About two years. I taught for three years, then realized if I wanted to stay sane, I'd better bail out."

"You were a teacher?" It wasn't the first occupation he'd have thought of for her.

"Yes. Third grade."

He smiled. Grade school. Now that made sense. Kids probably loved her.

"What?" She cocked her head at him. "What are you smiling about?"

Cam saw no suspicion on her face, only curiosity. It was good to see her looking more relaxed. When he'd first taken her into his arms, she'd held herself way too stiffly for him to be able to lead easily. She'd avoided his eyes, too. But she was loosening up. Keeping the conversation light clearly helped.

"Aren't I allowed to smile? Is that against class rules?" he teased.

She eyed him for a few more seconds. "Depends. If you're laughing at me, you have to go sit in the corner."

He grinned. "I was thinking that your teaching background explains your air of command."

Deborah arched a brow. "Are you calling me bossy?"

"Never." Cam watched her graceful movements. In spite of her arguments to the contrary, Deborah was a good dancer. He liked the feel of her in his arms. "How come you chose event planning?"

She sent him a small smile. "Maybe I wanted a career that would let me boss around adults instead of just kids."

Cam chuckled. "I hear your parties are all the rage among the younger crowd."

"Where do you hear that?" She looked as if she really wanted to know, and he remembered that she was building clientele and probably trying to track the success of her advertising techniques. His own party was going so well, so *professionally,* that it was easy to forget Deborah was new to planning business functions.

"My assistant, Barb, has grandchildren."

Deborah nodded. "I like Barb. Well, anyway, I've been lucky. And once I build a corporate clientele, I'll be able to choose the events I want to plan. I really enjoy kids' parties, but I'd love to kiss weddings goodbye."

"I can see how weddings might not excite you lately." *Hell.* He shouldn't have said that. Still, she seemed to be taking her broken engagement in stride, a lot better than he would in her place. Not that he would ever be in her place, since he planned to never get married and therefore never get engaged.

"Not because of Mark," she said, looking so un- fazed that he relaxed. "It's because weddings are a nightmare to plan. Everyone has so much invested emotionally in them. Every detail has to be perfect, right down to the shade of the bows on the candela- bra. One time the bride threw a tantrum because there were delphiniums in the altar bouquet and she hated delphiniums. Of course, she hadn't given the florist that little piece of info."

Cam murmured something appropriate, but he didn't want to talk about weddings. The mere thought of them sent chills down his spine.

Happily ever after. What a load of bunk.

"I hope to never plan another wedding in my life," Deborah said. "Except for my own, that is. Unlike you, I'm not afraid of marriage." Her incredibly big, incredibly blue eyes locked onto his.

Cam shifted his gaze. And found himself staring down at her cleavage. Which was much better defined than he would have guessed previously. She clearly had no idea that when she leaned toward him at that angle, he could see a lot of rounded breast and even a hint of a lacy black bra.

Cam swallowed. He jerked his gaze up. What were they talking about? Oh, yeah, marriage and fear. He couldn't let her get away with a crack like that.

He smiled back at her. "I'm not afraid, either." Horrified, yes, like at any other surefire losing bet. But not afraid. No, at this moment he was afraid only of losing control right here and now.

This dance was not a good idea.

Especially since he could tell that Deborah had noticed his interest in the neckline of her dress. Her cheeks had pinkened and she was holding herself stiffly again, as if he might haul her off and make love to her at any moment. An appealing idea, but socially unacceptable.

Damn.

What was he going to do? The woman had cast some kind of spell on him. For weeks he'd been unable to get the ingenue Deborah out of his head. Now she was a siren instead, and the situation had gone from bad to worse.

They were totally wrong for each other. Any idiot could see that. Free spirits like Deborah went merrily on their way, inconveniencing other people. And, in her case, talking their ears off in the process. Good Lord, that woman could talk. If he had to listen to her chatter very often, he'd be certifiable. He'd go absolutely nuts.

Cam drew in a sharp breath. *Nuts.* Yes. That was it.

"What's wrong?" Deborah asked. "Did I step on you? Are you okay?" Her brow creased in concern, she peered down at his foot.

His mind in a fog, Cam stared at her. "What are you talking about?"

"You stopped dancing."

"Oh. Right. Sorry." He took up the rhythm again, but only part of his brain was paying any attention to what his feet were doing. The rest of his brain was congratulating him on a brilliant idea.

It was the perfect solution to both of his problems.

Overexposure could work miracles. It was a no-fail way of getting Deborah out of his system. Several weeks of listening to her chatter—to say nothing of her music—would get rid of these inappropriate fantasies. His mind would go on automatic reject.

His social life, on the other hand, would steam ahead.

Cam wanted to laugh out loud in triumph. His two biggest problems, solved in one totally foolproof stroke.

Just to be on the safe side, he went over the idea again, carefully looking for potential weaknesses. But all he found were strengths.

All he had to do was get Deborah to agree. And he suspected he knew exactly how to achieve that.

"How's your search for corporate clients going?" he asked casually.

She grimaced. "Slowly. Everyone wants experience. Which, of course, I'll have after tonight, so maybe I'll make faster progress."

"I know of an excellent way for you to nab some corporate clients," he told her.

Her brows rose. "You do?" She sounded interested but wary.

"Yes, I do." Cam met and held her gaze. "You can agree to be my official social partner."

Chapter Six

Social partner? That sounded... Well, way too *social*, for starters. Especially coming from a man who lived in a totally different world than she did. For long seconds, Deborah could only stare at Cameron.

She couldn't have heard right. He had to have meant something else, only she couldn't think what that something else could be.

In fact, she couldn't think, period.

Why did this man always turn her mind to mush? It was a shame, it really was. If the idea weren't so ridiculous, she would swear Cameron's single goal in life was to disconcert her at every possible turn. And tonight he didn't have to work very hard, either, because the sight of him in black-and-white evening dress disrupted her concentration and did strange things to her pulse. So did the way he looked at her, his eyes intent.

Why had she thought he hadn't noticed her dress?

He was clearly waiting for her to say something, so Deborah did her best. "I'm not sure I heard you right."

"I said I'd like you to be my social partner, for want of a better term." He chuckled. "And I'm not suggesting anything improper, so you can lower your eyebrows again. The fact is, I need someone to go to social events with me, and you need contacts,'' he explained, as reasonably as if he made suggestions like this one every day. "This is the ideal solution."

She *had* heard right. Surprise almost made her miss the fact that the music had slowed and the lights dimmed. Uh-oh, here came a touchy-kissy number. Time to get off the dance floor.

Deborah tried to pull away, but Cameron only pulled her closer, planting his warm hand in the middle of her bare back and effectively robbing her of breath. "We should talk about this now, while we have the chance."

She swallowed. "You're asking me to go to parties, dances, that kind of thing with you?" He was kidding. Wasn't he?

"Right." He gave her an encouraging smile. "Just think of all the potential clients you'll meet."

That was for sure. Socializing would be far more effective than any advertising she could buy, even assuming she could afford advertising any time soon. Personal contact would probably cut her clientele-building time in half. It was an exciting offer. It was an unbelievable offer.

Except...

"Why would you be willing to do that for me?" Deborah pulled back slightly and looked up at him, trying to ignore the closeness of his firm, smooth-looking jaw. She could feel the heat from his body and smell the subtle, spicy aftershave he wore. Dancing with him felt intimate yet at the same time strangely comfortable. Not many men were built on a scale that complemented her height.

Suddenly Deborah realized Cameron hadn't answered her question. Maybe she should rephrase it. "What do you get out of the arrangement?"

"I told you. I get somebody I can count on to go with me to functions that aren't always exactly riveting." His eyes met hers but then slid away, leaving her with the sudden suspicion that he wasn't being entirely truthful. Oh, she could believe what he'd said was true. She just wondered what he had left out. Because the fact was, this man could undoubtedly get just about any woman he wanted to go with him. She hadn't noticed any shortage of female acquaintances.

"I thought your girlfriends went with you," Deborah said after a moment. Yes, *girlfriends,* plural. It was a good idea to remind herself that this man attracted women the way executives attracted business cards: in great number and without even trying. And she wasn't interested in being added to any collection.

He lifted one dark brow. "Sometimes I take a girlfriend, yes. But women can get the wrong idea. And in any case, I don't have a girlfriend anymore, remember?"

Deborah eyed him thoughtfully. His expression was the same one she'd seen several times before, the one she'd always thought of as his supercilious look.

Except maybe she'd misinterpreted that expression. Maybe he was embarrassed, instead.

Which he should be.

"Oh, I get it," Deborah said. "This is about all the girlfriends you've broken up with and the fact that you're too scared to marry any of them, isn't it?"

Cameron's brows jerked together. "No, it isn't."

"Really? You obviously want somebody safe to take to these functions, someone who won't make demands. If you weren't scared of commitment, I doubt you'd be so worried about women getting the wrong idea.''

His frown intensified. "That's damned ridiculous.''

He was annoyed with her now. Well, at least she'd succeeded in changing the mood. Lowered lights and dreamy music were all very well and good, but if she'd melted into a puddle at his feet, that would have given everyone way too much to talk about. And they already had more than enough, judging by the looks she and Cameron had been getting this evening.

The music changed again, and this time when she pulled away, Cameron let her. It was a good thing, too, because she couldn't afford to dance with him anymore. She needed a temptation she could handle, like the chocolate torte that awaited her back at their table. It was a lot safer than Cameron's arms. She also needed a clear head, and although this man inspired a lot of feelings in her, clearheadedness was not one of them.

Which was why she was nuts to even be considering his proposal.

On the other hand, how many times did opportunities like this one present themselves? As a business owner, she would be a fool to pass up the chance to meet a large number of potential corporate clients. After all, people liked having faces to attach to company names. They were a lot more likely to hire somebody they'd met.

That being the case, she shouldn't let the prospect of spending a little social time with Cameron Lyle scare her off. So she found him attractive. Big deal. He was still a guy with a commitment problem. Which explained why he wanted her, a woman patently unsuitable for him, to be his escort. He was an emotional coward and therefore not someone she could be seriously interested in.

And although she'd noticed a frankly sexual gleam in his eyes a couple of times tonight, it was probably only a reflex. Some men jingled their pocket change. Others adjusted their watches. Cameron flirted with women. All she had to do was keep her business goals firmly fixed in her mind, and everything would be fine.

She could handle him.

"SO DO WE HAVE A DEAL?" Cam asked as he watched Deborah make short work of her chocolate torte. Their table partners were all either dancing or mingling, enjoying the party. As he himself would be if he weren't so irritated with the way their conversation on the dance floor had ended.

It figured Deborah would want to know what he'd be getting out of the arrangement if she accompanied him as he proposed. He'd hoped she would snap up the business opportunity and not worry about anything else, but he should have known better.

And he should have answered her question a lot better.

Now she thought he wanted her along so he could avoid getting involved with a woman again. Nothing could be further from the truth. Just because he didn't believe in marriage didn't mean he wasn't open to the idea of a relationship. He couldn't guarantee how long it would last, of course, since passion was a notoriously fickle thing. Furthermore, he wasn't interested in any more relationships with women who spent all their time shopping and applying makeup.

But the mere fact that he'd become more discriminating lately did not mean he was scared of getting involved.

For a moment Cam contemplated pointing this out to Deborah, but he decided against it. Letting her think he'd asked her to be his escort because he was running from other women was a lot better than having her suspect his real reason. In all likelihood, an honest *I plan to get you out of my system by letting your chatter drive me up the wall* wouldn't go over very well.

Her long silence made him uneasy. Could she possibly have failed to recognize what a sterling business opportunity he was handing her? Or had her chocolate torte knocked her brain cells out of commission?

"Well?" Cam asked finally.

"I'm thinking," she told him in tones that were not encouraging.

He sighed. "Look, I'm sorry I scowled at you." Of course, if she insisted on psychoanalyzing people, she had to expect a little irritation from time to time. However, he did want her to agree to his suggestion, so why antagonize her?

Deborah shrugged. "I shouldn't have baited you. Your breakups aren't any of my business." Her tone implied she had a lot better things to do with her time. But the look she gave him didn't match her tone. Her quick glance held both awareness and discomfort. It was obvious that talking to him about man-woman relationships disturbed her.

"I can give you a definite *maybe*," Deborah said. "There are a few things I need to know before I decide. Let's talk about this after the party, okay? We both have a lot we should be doing right now."

Cam wanted to object, to insist that she tell him *yes* and do it now, but he controlled himself. She was right. They both needed to concentrate on their guests. Besides, he wasn't waiting with bated breath for her answer. It wasn't that big a deal. If she refused, he would figure out something else.

No sweat.

Even if his social life did get boring again.

DEBORAH SPENT the rest of the evening talking and laughing with Cameron's guests. On one level, she enjoyed herself immensely, which was a huge surprise. Who'd have thought she would find Cameron's friends and associates so interesting? They covered a much wider range of personalities and professions than she could ever have guessed. By the time she had talked with an artist, a policewoman and a scientist, she was ready to concede that she'd been unfair in assuming all his acquaintances would be boring business and society types.

On another level, however, panic hit her. What would she say to Cameron when he demanded her answer at the end of the evening? Like a race car zooming endlessly around a track, her brain kept covering the same territory.

This was an unbelievable business opportunity.

This was just plain unbelievable.

This was disaster waiting to happen.

By the end of the party, Deborah still hadn't made up her mind. It would have been a lot easier if she hadn't wimped out earlier. Hadn't she intended to say *yes?* Of course she had. So why, at the last minute, had she trotted out that coy little *maybe,* as if she were a panic-stricken sixteen-year-old who couldn't decide if she dared to date the hunky upperclassman?

Maybe because that was exactly how she felt. After all, who else did she know who regularly attended black-tie parties, formal dances and thousand-dollar-per-plate charity fund-raisers?

Fund-raisers.

Good grief. Why hadn't she thought of that before?

Imagine the money she could raise for Kids First if she moved in Cameron's circles. In only a few months, she could probably help her favorite charity more than she'd been able to in the past five years combined. How could she have the perfect means of helping out right here at her fingertips and then refuse to take advantage of it?

She couldn't.

CAM STOOD at the door with Deborah as they waved off the last group of guests. He smiled and said all the right things, but his brain was on automatic pilot, as it had been ever since Deborah had given him her definite *maybe.*

Much as he hated to admit it, he couldn't remember the last time he'd been this anxious about anything. It made no sense. Every day of the week, he made millions of dollars worth of financial decisions for clients. Yet he was biting his nails, at least figuratively, over a woman's decision about whether or not to go out with him. Of course, they wouldn't actually be going out, in the truest sense. They wouldn't be dating, kissing or—

Cam swallowed. He wasn't going to think about what else they wouldn't be doing.

He closed his front door more firmly than he'd intended. The little slam echoed in the entryway as he and Deborah came back in from the cold.

Cam sneaked a glance at Deborah. She looked as fresh as she had at the beginning of the party. Looking at her, nobody would guess it was well after midnight. Even her upswept hair still looked impeccable, although one little blond curl had escaped and nestled at the nape of her neck. It was alluring as hell, but thoughts like that one were off-limits, especially if he was going to wind up spending a lot of time with Deborah.

If. That was the big question.

But he wasn't going to ask it.

Damned right he wasn't. He'd already prompted her once and gotten a cool little *I'm thinking* for his pains. So he would let her think. Deborah was not the kind of woman who responded well to persuasion. She was too stubborn for that. She would tell him when she was ready. Meanwhile he should go compliment the caterer, the bartender and the musicians one more time. Then he should check for any items his guests might have left behind. He should also shut off the outdoor lights. In fact, there was a whole long list of things he should be doing.

"Have you decided?" Cam asked.

Hell.

Deborah looked at him, surprise in her huge blue eyes. "Oh, yeah, I have. I'll do it," she said, and immediately disappeared into the kitchen.

Cam slapped a hand to his forehead. This woman was going to kill him. If she didn't manage it with her stubbornness, she'd do it with her Let's-give-Cam-heart-failure-just-for-the-heck-of-it approach to life.

The woman was a menace.

And he had months of this to go.

Cam tracked Deborah into the kitchen and found her sinking a fork into a slice of chocolate torte.

"Look at all this great food you've got left over," she told him, looking and also sounding a lot more enthusiastic about the food in question than she'd been about his sterling business offer.

Cam fought irritation. What had he expected? That she would loudly praise him to the heavens for offering her such a tremendous opportunity? If she had, he would probably only be uncomfortable, because he knew damned well that helping her build clientele was not his main motivation.

"We need to talk," he reminded her as calmly as he could.

"Okay. Like I said, I accept your offer, although I should warn you that you might regret it."

Cam stifled a triumphant smile. "Trust me, I won't."

Freedom. Sweet freedom.

Deborah was lounging against his kitchen counter. She did a lot for white tile. His counter looked much better with green silk draped over it. Especially when Deborah wore the silk. She looked both sexy and perfectly comfortable. In fact, she looked ready to continue their conversation right here.

But he wasn't. There was no way he was talking over the details while the caterer and all her cleanup crew looked on, or at the very least, listened in. "Bring your cake into my study," he suggested, and was relieved when she followed him with no argument.

Cam had never realized how intimate his study

could be. Possibly that was because he didn't usually bring a woman into it in the wee hours of the morning. Especially not a woman enjoying chocolate torte the way Deborah was. She didn't merely eat it. She savored it. She chewed slowly and with great concentration. Occasionally her eyes closed and an expression of pure bliss spread over her features.

Cam cleared his throat. "I'd like to clarify a couple of points."

"I would, too." She seemed in no hurry, though. She took another bite of her cake, touching the fork to lips that were glossy and red.

Hypnotized, Cam stared at her mouth. Right from the beginning, he'd noticed Deborah had really great lips. Full and rosy. Tonight they were off-the-scale great.

"But you go first." With a delicate sweep of her tongue, Deborah licked chocolate off her full lower lip.

Cam stifled a groan. What had he done? He could feel it right now, his entire plan was going to be a bust. How was he supposed to get this woman out of his thoughts when she sat there eating cake like... like...*that?*

This was impossible.

But he couldn't change his mind. They'd already made the deal. Besides, it wasn't an insurmountable problem. Okay, Deborah Clark was a beautiful woman, and he was strongly attracted to her. So what? He'd been attracted to plenty of women before without acting on that attraction. He could control himself.

"I wanted to talk to you about clothes," Cam said.

"Since you'll need several dresses you wouldn't otherwise have to buy, I want to pay—"

"No," said Deborah. Small chinks of silver on china and china on wood punctuated her response as she set her chocolate torte, unfinished, on the end table.

"I insist." Dammit, this woman was the most stubborn female he'd ever met. When he'd first gotten mixed up with her, he'd had no clue how obstinate she could be. She'd metamorphosed from a cheery, flippant girl into a tempting, intractable woman.

But at least she'd stopped torturing him with the cake.

"Look, we don't have to shop together," he said. "Just give me the bills and I'll reimburse you."

She laughed, a little wildly, it seemed to Cam. "You mean, you've decided you don't need to supervise?"

He not only didn't need to, he didn't trust himself to. It was a good thing Deborah turned out to have impeccable taste, because watching her model barely-there dresses would probably give him a heart attack.

"I'm sure I'll be happy with whatever you choose."

"I appreciate your trust, but the answer is still no. Thank you, but no." Her eyes told him she meant it. "I will buy my own clothes."

When he started to protest, Deborah held up one hand in a way that reminded him she'd been a teacher, even if briefly. "This will be an investment for me. I'm sure I'll need evening clothes once my business takes off. Speaking of which, I need to know the dates of these social commitments. That way I can put them on my calendar. I'll drop by your office some time next week, okay?"

"Fine." Cam knew she was changing the subject, and he let her. But he hadn't conceded defeat yet. He would just have to work on her, that was all.

"One other thing," Deborah said. She shifted a little. "If you meet someone and want to take her to these events instead of me, don't hesitate to tell me. I wouldn't want to be in the way."

Cam looked at her uncharacteristically earnest face and almost smiled. "It's not going to happen, but thanks, anyway. And of course the same goes for you. Feel free to back out if you need to."

"You say it won't happen as if it's an impossibility. But what if you fell in love, just like that?" Deborah snapped her fingers.

He laughed. "Impossible even to imagine. For me, thinking about love is like thinking about dragons or the tooth fairy."

A pucker formed between her brows. "I don't get it. What do you mean?"

"I mean none of them exist. So it's pointless to think about them."

She looked shocked. Cam could almost swear he saw her pupils dilate. He hoped she wasn't going to faint. Fortunately she was now sitting on his leather couch, so if she did keel over, he'd at least have somewhere to put her.

"You don't believe in love." Deborah said it slowly, like she was trying to fathom it. And then apparently she figured it out, because her expression changed and suddenly she was looking at Cam as if she'd made a major discovery about him.

He didn't even want to think about what that might be.

"Romantic love, as in between a couple? No." He'd seen no convincing evidence of it. And all around him were examples to the contrary, including the majority of his friends. Not to mention his parents. Three marriages apiece. Thank God they'd finally given up.

"I guess you realize you're very much in the minority." Deborah had a challenging look on her face. "Consider how much has been written about love over the centuries. And by so many people."

He smiled. "A lot has been written about Camelot, too, but that doesn't mean it exists."

She nodded, as if she'd expected him to make an argument like that. "So I assume you don't believe in marriage, either."

"Right."

"That explains why everyone says you're planning to never marry."

Cam shot her a sharp glance. "Everyone? Who, everyone?"

She grinned. "Just about everyone in Tulip Tree Square, that's who."

Cam eyed her. She was enjoying this, the little tease. She was having a field day telling him about the gossip going around their small corner of town. Gossip about him.

Damn. A certain amount of speculation about his love life and the women he dated was inevitable. But this was too much. And he knew exactly who to blame.

Barb.

"Since you don't believe in love, that must make life very dull for you," said Deborah.

"No. After all, I do believe in passion." *Hell, yes.* His gaze lingered on her full red mouth. Cam saw her cheeks pinken and smiled. "I also believe in instant sexual attraction or magnetism, whatever you want to call it. And I believe in affection. But love..." He shook his head. "I think romantic love is a term used to describe what is really passion. Love sounds better."

"Cynic."

"I'm not surprised you believe in love, though," he said. "I'd expect as much from someone with your optimistic, rose-colored view of life."

Deborah only smiled. But she said nothing, and the small surge of disappointment he felt made Cam aware of how much he enjoyed matching verbal wits with her. It made him aware of other things, too.

Even though his main goal was to get this woman out of his system, he would have a lot of fun in the process.

Chapter Seven

"Hi, Ann, how's it going?" Deborah plunked herself down on her usual stool and inhaled deeply. "What smells so great?" As usual, Sweetness and Light had the best quality air for miles around.

Her friend shrugged. "At a guess, it's either the quiches or the English sausage rolls. Can't say for sure, thanks to this blasted cold."

"So that's why you're wearing that funny little mask."

"It's also why I'm washing my hands approximately twenty times per minute." Ann sounded exasperated.

"Why don't you get someone else into the kitchen and spend the day doing paperwork instead?" Deborah suggested.

"Because I don't have anyone to fill in. Good thing I'm still standing, since half my staff is out with the flu."

"*The* flu?"

"The very same," Ann confirmed.

"Oh, no."

Indianapolis had been hit hard with an upper-respiratory flu that left its victims weak and aching for days. Symptoms were drastic enough to make the malady the number one topic of conversation, superceding even the weather, which was as cold and snowy as usual for early February.

Deborah shook her head. She should have something practical to offer, like the help Ann was so desperately short of. But Ann wouldn't want her help. Her friend would undoubtedly rather risk any number of catering glitches than jeopardize her business reputation by letting Deborah near a kitchen. And who could blame her? Few people managed feats like boiling hot dogs until both they *and* the saucepan were charred beyond recognition.

"When are you going to let me teach you to cook?" Ann's thoughts obviously followed a related path as she cut vegetables into julienne strips with enviable speed.

Deborah grinned. "Never, if I can help it." She grazed on a couple of carrot strips Ann handed her. "You know I'll help any way I can, but I think you underestimate how much I hate cooking. And you have to admit, a three-legged donkey would show more aptitude than I do."

"You just need the right attitude."

"Uh-huh." Deborah crossed her arms. "I guess that's why you gave me those napkins that say 'Dinner Will Be Ready When The Fire Alarm Goes Off,' right?" She used one of those napkins whenever she needed a quick chuckle. Which, lately, had been pretty often. In the ten days since she'd agreed to this social partnership arrangement with Cameron, Deborah had suffered one crisis of confidence after another. It wasn't like her to worry, and that fact made her worry even more.

Then there was the irritation she felt every time she remembered how Cameron kept trying to buy her clothing, like he did for all those women he dated and discarded.

She was *not* a disposable date.

It was a good thing Cameron had been out of town almost the entire ten days since his party. Who knew what shape she'd be in if she had to deal with him face-to-face.

Ann was shaking her head. "I gave you those napkins to remind you that reading while cooking is usually a mistake. But maybe none of that matters. If this thing with Cameron Lyle works out, you won't have to cook, anyway."

"What *thing?* There is no *thing* with Cameron Lyle. I told you, this is a business arrangement." Deborah said it slowly and clearly, just in case Ann was suffering from another of her periodic bouts with deafness.

Ann shrugged. "I heard you. All my customers heard you, too. But I was in that kitchen with you, remember? It was the end of Cameron's party, and you two looked all set for a private party of your own, if you know what I mean."

"That's ridiculous."

"Deny it all you want, but my vibes tell me something's up." Ann piped deviled egg mixture into egg halves. "So what are you wearing to this Valentine's Day affair?"

"Don't your vibes tell you that, too?"

Her friend pulled a face. At least, Deborah thought she did. It was hard to tell through the mask.

"I have no idea what I'm wearing," Deborah told her.

Ann pulled off her mask and gaped at her. "But it's this weekend. Five days away. As black tie as they come, and at Indy's most elegant hotel. In fact, according to Stella, this thing is the biggest social event of the winter."

"I know all that." The butterflies she got just thinking about it irritated her. "I'll dig up something." If she admitted she was going shopping, Ann would only make a bigger deal out of it.

"The green dress you wore to Cameron's party is the only formal gown you own," her friend pointed out with the authority of one who knew. "You've got nothing at all to wear to this affair."

Deborah winced. If only Ann would stop using the word *affair*.

"The way I see it, you'll have to go shopping," Ann said.

Deborah tried to look innocent. "Yeah, I guess so." And she'd buy the most stunning dress she found. She deserved it, for putting up with all the worry that she would publicly disgrace herself by spilling champagne, forgetting people's names or hitting Cameron over the head.

Ann's eyes lit up. "Great! I'll go with you."

"Only if you promise not to talk me into buying anything else," Deborah warned. Her closet was filled with "absolutely perfect on you" hats, scarves and shoes, each covered with ten layers of dust. "Leave your evil shopaholic twin at home."

"I will, I will. You have nothing to worry about."

Deborah rolled her eyes.

CAM ACCEPTED the letter Barb gave him, signed it and handed it back to her. "Are you sure you're feeling okay?'' he asked. ''You still look a little pale. Why don't you go home early and get some rest? It's almost four-thirty, anyway.'' He himself had only just gotten back in town, and he'd almost skipped coming to the office in favor of putting his feet up at home.

''I'm fine, thanks. Finally.'' Barb grimaced. ''The worst part of this darned flu was having to miss your party. Did you take pictures?''

Cam smiled. It figured Barb would ask that. Every conceivable space in his assistant's office was taken up by snapshots of her children and grandchildren. If Barb had been at his party, he'd now be deluged by photos. They'd be good ones, too, because in addition to being enthusiastic, Barb had talent. One of her nature shots hung on his office wall.

''I didn't, but Deborah hired a photographer,'' Cam said. ''I'm sure she'll show you the proofs when they come back.''

''She's already said she will. Such a nice girl.'' Barb smiled. ''It's wonderful of you to help her out by hiring her.'' Cheerful brown eyes twinkled at him.

Cam felt his face warm. He murmured something noncommittal, wondering as he did what Barb would say if she knew about his recent arrangement with Deborah. He wasn't going to tell her, of course. The last thing he needed was to have his assistant congratulating herself on having played matchmaker.

Any intelligent man could tell Deborah was the sort of woman who expected involvement to lead to marriage. Since the mere thought of marriage was enough to bring Cam out in hives, he and Deborah were not a match made in heaven.

Which reminded him...

"How did news travel all over Tulip Tree Square that I've got no intention of ever getting married?"

Barb shrugged. "I might've mentioned our bet to a few folks."

"Our bet?"

"Yes. The one we made at Stella's wedding last summer, remember? I bet you ten bucks you'd be married within two years, and you agreed to pay me fifty if you *ever* married."

"Oh, yeah." When would he learn not to get into conversations like that with Barb? "Well, did you have to spread it around?"

"I only told a couple of people. Who said everyone knows?" Barb asked.

"Deborah."

"Ah…"

Cam frowned at her. "What does *Ah…* mean?"

"Nothing. I think it's interesting that the topic came up, that's all. Hey, where are you going?"

"I have work to do," he told her. "You know, the stuff one does at one's desk, besides talking on the phone."

She ignored that, probably because he told her too often how good she was at her job. He'd have to stop doing that. No more compliments, no more raises every six months.

"I haven't finished with you yet. You owe me details," Barb said.

"Details?" He flinched, but then Cam realized Barb wasn't talking about Deborah. Relief hit him.

"Right," Barb said. "First I'm sick, then you go out of town for days on end. Now that I finally get to talk to you, I want to hear all about it."

"Oh. Well, as I'm sure you heard, my whole living

room metamorphosed into a winter park," he told her. Cam was in the middle of his description when the office door flew open and Deborah stormed in.

"What in the Sam Hill is this?" She waved a white box. Her cheeks were flushed as deep a pink as the leggings she wore, and her eyes flashed. Her blond hair nearly crackled with energy. She looked vibrant and beautiful.

And sexy. Very sexy. Temper suited her.

Cam stifled a smile. Maybe he should try putting her in one more often.

"It looks like a dress box." Aware of Barb's avid stare, he ushered Deborah into his office and shut the door.

"I know it's a dress box. It has a dress in it," Deborah said in slow, pseudo-patient tones. "The question is, what was it doing outside my door?"

"You weren't home when I came by." Of course that wasn't what she meant, but it was fun to see the look on her face. This woman had provided him with one hell of a lot of frustration lately. Why not return the favor?

It was good to be home.

Deborah put her hands on her hips. "Why did you buy it for me?"

"Because I thought it suited you. Was I wrong? I know not every woman likes red." Deborah would look fantastic in it, though. He'd had no time to deliver it to her before leaving town, but he'd had nine days of interesting—and very hot—daydreams about Deborah wearing that dress.

She glared at him. "That's not the point. I already told you, I'm fully capable of buying my own clothes, and that's what I'm going to do."

"I thought we could compromise and each buy a few dresses." Civility demanded that he at least try to talk to her in a reasonable manner. Civility also required that he *not* do what he really wanted to do, which was haul her into his arms and kiss her.

All things considered, civility was a real drag.

Her full lips set in mutinous lines. "I'm not accepting clothes from you. It's not appropriate."

"Of course it is. You're going to these events to help me out, so the least I can do is provide some of the clothes you'll need. Think of it as a uniform." Cam shrugged. "Or, if it makes you feel better, don't keep the dress. Just wear it and then give it back to me."

She gave him a blank look. "But then you couldn't return it and get your money back."

Cam could feel his patience dissolving. "I don't care about that. I don't want to return the dress, anyway. I'll give it to charity. You might as well wear it once before I do."

For a moment Deborah looked like she was considering that idea, but then she shook her head. "No. Take it back. Now." With that, she deposited the box on his desk, whirled around and vanished.

Cam stood in the middle of his office. He could hear Deborah saying something chatty to Barb, but before long the front door closed and the office was quiet. Too quiet. He had about ten seconds before the beginning of the Great Inquisition. Cam started to count.

He'd gotten to nine when the knock came at his door.

HALF AN HOUR LATER, Deborah opened her door and found Cameron outside it. He was holding the white dress box.

"Oh, it's you," she said without enthusiasm. Which was rude, but what did he expect when he'd obviously come up to her apartment to continue their argument? She wasn't in the mood for any more arguing. All she wanted was some late afternoon tea and cookies to recharge her batteries.

On the other hand, they might as well get this issue settled once and for all. With a sigh, Deborah stepped back to let Cameron in.

"I'm not going to return this." He indicated the box.

When she opened her mouth to suggest an impolite alternative, he shook his head. "Hear me out, okay?"

Reluctantly, she waited.

"I don't want to return this, because the shop I bought it from is a small one. Its owner depends on regular business from her customers."

"Especially her biggest customers, like you." Deborah bit her lip. Why had she said that? It was a petty, snippy comment. Plus, it made her sound like she had a personal interest in his spending habits, which she didn't.

Cameron raised a brow in a familiar gesture. "I doubt I'm one of her biggest customers. But I like to think I'm loyal, and I've shopped there for years."

She could believe it. How many thousands of dollars had Cameron spent on clothes for his various girlfriends? It was none of her business, of course. And her interest was purely academic. For all she cared, the man could buy dresses for fifty women every week of the year.

She wasn't going to be one of them.

"I like to support area merchants, and I like Stella, and that's why I don't want to return the dress," he said.

Deborah stared at him for a long moment. To say she was surprised would be an understatement. Who'd have guessed Cameron was this loyal? Or empathetic? He was generous, too, if he'd keep a useless dress rather than return it.

Once again the man had knocked her off-balance, and even though he was as imposing as ever standing in her tiny entryway, this time her discomfort had nothing to do with his physical presence. This time it was all about character, and he obviously had more of that than she'd given him credit for.

How else might she have misjudged him?

Cameron's green eyes were serious. "If you don't want to wear this dress, give it to a friend or relative, because I have no use for it." He pushed the box into her hands.

Deborah found herself holding it, and she stared down at the elegant box with its glossy gold lettering. "What about one of your lady friends?"

"I told you, I don't have a girlfriend." He sounded impatient.

"I know you don't have a *main* girlfriend, but I thought one of your other lady friends—"

She broke off, because this time, Cameron was the one staring at her. It wasn't a friendly stare, either. It was a stare that made her feel about ten inches high.

"What, you think I operate with a main girlfriend and a bunch of emergency backup girlfriends, is that it?"

Put that way, it did sound absurd. And insulting.

"You sure have a high opinion of me," he said.

Deborah saw something that looked very much like hurt in his eyes, and she felt a twinge of regret. She was annoyed with herself, too. Even if she didn't agree with how he conducted his love life, it was none of her business. Besides, for all she knew, his reputation might be based more on supposition and rumor than it was on fact. In any case, she couldn't let him think she despised him, because that wasn't true.

It was even less true now than it had been before.

"You have quite a reputation as a ladies' man, you know," Deborah said matter-of-factly. "That's all I meant."

He grimaced. "Yeah, well, these things get exaggerated all too easily. And while I'll admit to having had a few girlfriends, I've always had them one at a time."

She nodded. There was no reason not to believe him, and it was entirely plausible that what seemed like a lot of women all at once was actually a lot of women in rapid succession. After all, she'd already figured out that he didn't have long relationships.

Cameron sniffed the air. "Is something burning?"

"Oh, no!" Deborah wailed. "The milk!"

"MAYBE YOU SHOULD BUY an electric teakettle and warm the milk in the microwave," Cam suggested. "That would be easier, wouldn't it?"

"What you really mean is, then I might be able to have tea without burning the place down." Deborah grinned.

Cam smiled back. "Well...yes." He liked the humor in her eyes. He also liked her ability to laugh at herself. In his experience, it was fairly rare.

He took a sip of his Earl Grey tea. He was a coffee

person, but having helped Deborah with the boiled milk mess, he'd managed to wangle an invitation to afternoon tea, so the least he could do was drink the stuff. It wasn't bad. He'd never add warm milk to it, tradition or no tradition. But his own unadulterated tea was palatable, especially accompanied by tasty Swedish ginger cookies.

"I got them in a Christmas care package from my sister," Deborah said when he commented on them.

"Where does your sister live?"

"In Atlanta. She and her boyfriend moved there for his job. Julie's a writer, so she can live anywhere." Her smile was wistful.

"You miss her," he guessed.

"Of course I do. What about you? Brothers and sisters?"

Cam shook his head. "None." Good thing, too. Much as he'd have liked a sibling, he wouldn't wish parents like his on anyone else. They weren't bad people, just selfish. And completely unsuited to each other. Cam liked both his parents now that they were divorced. And now that he didn't have to live with them anymore.

Bad marriages made for really bad childhoods.

Cam glanced around Deborah's apartment. It looked much the same as it had the last time he'd seen it, right down to the cat snoozing on the sofa.

"Every time I see your cat, she's sleeping." Cam got out of the armchair and went over to peer at Libby. The cat didn't move so much as a muscle. Deborah followed him over and he felt his body tighten in instant awareness.

"She conserves her energy," Deborah said. "The

life of a house cat is a hectic one, you know, especially at night.''

Libby's ear twitched.

"Oh, right, the nocturnal hunt. Is that why she doesn't go out much? You're afraid of what she might bring in?''

Deborah shook her head. "There are several factors. The most important one is she can't climb trees.''

"Oh, I see. She's declawed.''

"No, Libby has all her claws. She just doesn't climb well.''

Cam stared at Deborah and then at Libby. "You're kidding.''

"No.'' Deborah sighed. "I practiced with her when she was a kitten, but I guess she's not climber material. I asked the vet about it and she didn't seem concerned.''

Cam had no trouble at all envisioning Deborah in discussion with the vet. She would have listened intently and asked all the pertinent questions. She would have taken down any instructions and followed them to the letter. His impression so far was that, for all her laid-back attitude toward life in general, Deborah Clark did not do anything halfway. When she undertook a project, she approached it with complete dedication and enthusiasm.

He'd bet his last dollar that she made love the same way.

Cam grimaced. Thoughts like these had to stop. How could he expect to get Deborah out of his system if he couldn't focus on the things that really mattered? Things like her chatter, for example.

Speaking of which, where was it?

Aside from a brief appearance at his party, it had all but disappeared. In fact, he hadn't heard Deborah's over-the-top chattiness in weeks. He'd been gone some of that time, true, but still…

"How come you're so quiet all of a sudden?" Cam asked.

Surprise filled her eyes. "Am I? Sorry. I'll try to be a better hostess." She looked faintly amused.

"I don't mean now, specifically. I mean lately," he explained.

Deborah stared at him blankly.

Cam tried again. "You're not talking nonstop anymore." Damn. Now he sounded accusing. Which was exactly how he felt. After all, he'd been counting on Deborah to chatter at him until his teeth hurt and he ran screaming in the opposite direction, never again entertaining a single erotic thought about the woman. Instead, she'd done everything *except* bore him, until his fantasizing had reached disturbing new levels. And it wasn't his teeth that hurt.

Deborah was chuckling. "Oh. Well, actually, I only gab when I'm nervous." Clearly anything but nervous now, she sat in a comfortable looking blue armchair with her legs curled up under her. Along with the hot pink leggings, she wore an ivory sweatshirt with eye-popping multicolored flowers on it.

Cam frowned. "I don't get it. Every single time our paths crossed, you talked my ear off—" He stopped when he saw her expression. "You were nervous? Of me?"

"What do you expect, walking around scowling all the time?" Suddenly her beautiful blue eyes held accusation. "You're very intimidating when you frown, you know. Besides, as I recall, every time you saw me you had some kind of complaint.''

Yeah, chiefly that you were wearing an engagement ring.

Cam frowned. He couldn't tell her that. Besides, all it meant was that he had dog-in-the-manger tendencies. Not an appealing idea.

''See?'' Deborah pointed at him. ''You're doing it again, and that's exactly what I mean.'' She shook her head slowly, like a teacher showing disappointment in a student. ''Look in the mirror some time, because that is not a friendly frown.''

''*Is* there such a thing as a friendly frown?''

''Of course. Not all frowns signal dislike or disapproval. There are thoughtful frowns, perplexed frowns and frowns of doubt.'' She illustrated each one after she'd listed it, and Cam had to admit he'd never seen a friendlier frowner. Not that that proved much, since Deborah probably couldn't look threatening if she tried. Her soft blond hair and open features were too wholesome. ''There are inquiring frowns,'' she continued. ''And sympathetic frowns—''

''Okay, I get the picture. So you were nervous of me because I frowned at you.''

''Yes, partly.'' Deborah said it almost absentmindedly, but then she looked uncomfortable.

''Partly? What else about me made you nervous?''

Her gaze shifted and settled on her cat. ''Never mind. It's not important.''

Cam knew then that, whatever it was, she had no intention of telling him. He also knew that if Deborah Clark only chattered when she was nervous, this was not good news for him. It meant he couldn't count on

Deborah to produce enough chatter to put him off her for good.

Damn.

Cam accepted another ginger cookie and munched it while he and Deborah chatted some more about Libby and other animals in the neighborhood. As he'd suspected, Deborah knew about all the pets, from old Mrs. Quigley's poodle to little Jeremy White's hamster. Moreover, Deborah knew whose dog was sick and whose cat just had kittens. It was both impressive and more than a little frightening. After all, if she knew this much about the neighborhood's animals, how much more might she know about its resident humans? About him?

It was a disconcerting thought, but it was nowhere near as troublesome as the problem involving Deborah's disappearing chatter. Now *that* was a significant setback.

But all was not lost. It was way too early to concede defeat, and at least he knew what he had to do.

Come up with Plan B.

DEBORAH CAME to a dead stop in front of the department store escalator. It was completely obvious why Ann wanted to go upstairs. She had a notorious weakness for lace-trimmed bits of nothing. And since this was an upscale store, it undoubtedly offered plenty. But Deborah couldn't afford to breathe the oh-so-tempting air up there.

"I am not buying any lingerie."

Ann frowned. "I thought you said you don't have a push-up bra."

"That's exactly what I said." Evil instruments of torture. No way would a woman have invented them.

"But you're going to need one."

Deborah raised a brow. Then the gesture reminded her of Cameron and she quickly lowered it again. "How do you know that? I haven't even found the dress yet."

"And that's another thing," Ann said. "I can't believe how many dresses you've nixed."

"You think I'm being too picky?"

"Yes. The party is two days away." Her friend's voice was heavy with emphasis.

"I know, and I'll find something. Eventually. Probably even today." Deborah smiled at her. Ann didn't know about the backup dress in Deborah's closet. The red one that she had reluctantly allowed Cameron to persuade her to keep on hand in case of emergency.

Emergency. As if she would ever consider the lack of a fancy dress an emergency. In her world, lack of rent money was an emergency. Lack of *groceries* was an emergency. It just went to show how far apart their worlds were.

As if she needed reminding.

Still, Cameron was obviously serious about not returning his purchase, so what was the difference if the beautiful red silk dress spent time livening up her closet before being donated wherever he planned to send it?

Deborah sighed. It was too bad she felt so strongly about not wearing any clothes Cameron bought. Because the red dress was the most gorgeous one she'd seen in a long time. Extremely simple, with only a few well-placed tucks and pleats, it draped beautifully. Deborah could vouch for that because she'd tried it on. Even in her anger, she'd been unable to resist. And she'd recognized the superb quality of the dress. The obvious expense of it made her even madder.

She had no intention of telling Ann about the dress. Furthermore, since she also had no intention of wearing it, she'd better get on the stick and find a dress she could wear. The trouble was, they were all so ordinary.

Especially compared with the red one.

"Come on," she told Ann. "We've got two very good stores left in this mall. I'm sure we'll find something in one of them. And then, if I absolutely have to wear a push-up bra with it, we'll go look at lingerie. Okay?"

"Okay. It'll all be worth it. Just wait and see."

ANN REPEATED those words the following day as Deborah gingerly parked herself in the hot seat at The Mane Event and submitted to comb, scissors and rollers. Actually, having her hair worked on was kind of relaxing as long as she didn't look in the mirror or pay too much attention to the giant locks of hair floating to the floor around her.

"You know, I can't remember the last time I did this," Deborah mused.

"Believe me, I know." Ann rolled her eyes. "Just promise me we've seen the last of the ponytails and shapeless tunic tops."

"I'll think about it."

"You have beautiful hair," said the technician, who was in her early twenties and wore a nose ring, but whose hair was attractively styled. "Natural highlights, plenty of body, just enough wave to hold a style well. I'll do some layering and texturizing, and maybe give you a little curl too, okay?"

"Okay." Whatever texturizing meant. Chances were, it would be an improvement. The salon had a good reputation.

Half an hour later, Deborah stared at herself in shock.

Her hair fell in soft, gleaming waves to her shoulders. She now had a very attractive hint of bangs. Layering corrected the heaviness of the hair around her face, making it wave more. Her eyes looked huge.

"Wow." Ann gaped at her. "How come my haircuts never do that much for me?"

"Because your hair is too short," Deborah said.

"Yes, but still..." Ann shook her head. "I've only got one thing to say."

"Which is...?"

"Look out, Cameron Lyle."

Chapter Eight

Cam nodded to one acquaintance and smiled across the hotel ballroom at another. Tonight no one was talking about business, which suited him fine. Better to enjoy the excellent music, striking Valentine's Day décor and lavish buffet table.

Watching Deborah take in their surroundings was more than half the fun. She'd scanned the place with eyes that didn't miss a thing, from the black-and-white checkerboard tile floor, to the huge white columns, to the flower bouquets, all of which were red. Cam could see her taking mental notes. Maybe she was writing them up right now, and that was why she was taking forever in the ladies' room.

Or maybe it just seemed like forever because the *zing* went out of the room as soon as Deborah left it.

Cam took a healthy swallow of his ice water. He wasn't allowed to think about *zing*. Tonight might be the most romantic night of the year, but Deborah was off-limits to him.

Off-limits.

As he'd reminded himself at least a dozen times in the hour since Plan B had popped into his head.

He shouldn't be thinking about plans tonight, no

matter how desperate he was to get Deborah out of his system. After two intense weeks of travel and consulting, followed by four long days of catching up at the office, he was exhausted.

Which was undoubtedly why the sight of Deborah this evening had made him totally lose his mind. He'd taken one look at her sexy new hairstyle and her classy, clingy black dress, and he'd immediately hit on Plan B.

Seduce her.

Taking Deborah Clark to bed would be one sure way to get her out of his system. Once he'd been to bed with a woman, the thrill of the chase was gone and so was the mystery.

Perfect.

Except he drew the line at seducing the young and the innocent.

Cam frowned.

On the other hand, Deborah wasn't all that young. She was twenty-seven, a fact that lately he'd found a lot more believable than he had when he'd first met her. And how innocent could she be, for Pete's sake? After all, she'd been engaged. What if he was just as wrong about her experience level as he'd been about her age? What if he missed out on something incredible, all because he was too inflexible in his thinking?

Besides, even if Deborah had very little experience of men, wasn't it time she acquired more? Who better to help her accomplish that than Cam, who made his intentions, or lack thereof, perfectly clear?

Cam grimaced. All this back-and-forth was giving him a headache. He should simply make his attraction clear and let Deborah decide. She was far from indifferent to him.

Maybe it was time to find out how far.

DEBORAH HURRIED out of the ladies' room. She should have worn the new bra Ann had finally persuaded her to buy—along with the matching bikini underwear. She didn't like the darned thing, but at least it would have made it through the evening. Now, one safety-pinned bra strap later, it was time to hurry back before she missed anything.

She was probably the only guest here who understood exactly how tough it was to produce stunning visual effects like tonight's. The huge backdrops featuring hundreds of gleaming gold pillar candles were the perfect wall ornamentation for the ballroom's black-and-white Art Deco 1930's era décor. And the floral arrangements were nothing short of ingenious. All were red, but each held only one type of flower: tulips, roses or gladioli.

All in all, the event was every bit as elegant as she'd expected, a complete triumph that benefited several worthy programs in local health services.

As soon as Deborah reentered the ballroom, she spotted Cameron. It wasn't hard, because he stood out in the crowd. He was younger than most of the other men and in considerably better shape. There was no softness to his physique, no signs of overindulgence in his face. He looked right at home in his surroundings. Wearing a charcoal suit and snowy white shirt, he was talking to a silver-haired gentleman at the opposite end of the room.

As she watched, his head lifted. Even from across the room, she could feel his gaze. Her pulse picked up speed.

Deborah swallowed and started across the room.

She could see how many women would misunderstand if he flirted with them. After all, Cameron had a sexy smile and gorgeous green eyes with very attractive crinkles at the corners. Even his nose was attractive, for heaven's sake. Aristocratic was the only word for a nose like that. It was a good thing his jaw was so formidable, or she might have risked joining the ranks of all the other gasping women. As it was, when he smiled at her and turned on the charm, all she had to do was remind herself that Valentine's Day meant little or nothing to a man as cynical as he was. A man, moreover, who was used to inspiring female admiration and equally used to getting his own way.

"There you are," Cameron greeted her. "Come meet Herb Landown." Introducing her to the surgeon, he watched them shake hands with an indulgent smile that made her want to grit her teeth.

"Deborah owns an event planning business," Cameron said.

Deborah kept her calm smile, but only with an effort. She felt like a child being introduced to the grown-ups at the party, especially when Cameron gave an enthusiastic description of the party she'd planned for him. He was helping her out with contacts, true, but she didn't need to be taken under anyone's wing.

Especially not Cameron's.

Dr. Landown looked impressed. His eyes held keen intelligence and a genuine interest. "I'm thinking about giving a costume party. Have you ever done one of those?"

"No, but I love costume parties. You could give guests a theme to work with."

"That's a great idea. Let me tell you a little more

about it, and we'll see if you might be interested in taking it on for me.''

By the time they left Herb Landown chatting with another doctor who had hailed him, Deborah was happier than she'd been in weeks. This party was not at all the stiff kind of event she'd been worried about. Also, the prospect of gaining another client always cheered her, and she particularly liked the surgeon. She felt like singing right along with the Duke Ellington tune the band was playing. Even the sight of Cameron's satisfied grin didn't spoil her mood.

''You were quite a hit,'' he remarked as they headed for the buffet table.

''It wasn't anything I did. It was you, raving about the party I planned for you.''

He shook his head. ''That's not true. You're so enthusiastic about what you do, and people respond to that. I'm betting Landown will hire you to plan that July party of his.''

''Maybe. That reminds me. One of the guests at your party hired me a few days later, but you were out of town and I couldn't thank you. So I'm thanking you now.''

''You're welcome. Which guest is that?'' He put his hand on her back to guide her through a cluster of people.

''Hazel Myers.'' If only she weren't so aware of his warm hand in the middle of her bare back. Next time she bought a dress for one of these functions, it would have long sleeves and a high neckline, both front and back.

''No kidding?'' Cameron pursed his lips in a whistle. ''That's a coup. She must have been really impressed. Congratulations.''

"Thanks." Deborah would have savored the compliment except that out of the corner of her eye, she saw a familiar face. She felt her stomach drop the equivalent of ten floors.

The evening had suddenly gotten a lot more complicated.

"What's the matter?" Cameron asked.

"Marilyn's here. Marilyn Snyder," she reminded him. "Mark's mother, who thinks I'm involved with you." The woman she loved dearly and would ordinarily be thrilled to run into at a party. Deborah sighed. This was what came of fibbing.

"Ah, yes." He shrugged. "I don't see the problem. After all, you're here with me."

"Yes, but I'm not really *with* you, if you know what I mean." Deborah flushed. Great. Now he would think she was hinting that she wanted his attention. Why wouldn't he think that, based on his success rate with women?

"She won't know that, certainly not from me." Cameron gave her a slow, sexy smile as he put his arm around her.

Once again, little tingles shot through her wherever their skin touched. Deborah closed her eyes. It was going to be a long evening.

"HAVE YOU SEEN the conservatory they just added on to this hotel?" Cam asked two hours later. It was time to escape for a while. Deborah was a trouper, but he vividly remembered her telling him she didn't enjoy parties. After nearly three hours of circulating and chatting, the strain was beginning to show. She needed a break.

So did he. He wanted some time alone with Deborah.

"No, I haven't seen it," she said.

"It's the finest conservatory around," he told her. "They've got an incredible variety of tropical and subtropical plants, including some sea grape trees and a spectacular Royal poinciana." Cam stopped. Any minute now, he'd be spouting off Latin names and launching into a monologue about what was on the left and on the right.

The truth was, he felt unsure of Deborah's mood. He wasn't used to women he couldn't read, and it bothered him to realize he had no idea at all what Deborah was thinking right now. She looked remote, not at all like the open, cheerful girl he'd thought she was. Or the passionate woman he now suspected she really was.

"Sounds good," Deborah commented.

Without another word, Cam led her out of the ballroom, down the hallway and into the conservatory. They followed stone pathways through lush foliage. Judging by the faint murmurs he could hear, there were a few other people in the glass-domed facility. But the gentle splash of the fountain at the center of the conservatory covered up most sounds, and Cam couldn't see anyone through the dense foliage. For all intents and purposes, they were alone.

Finally.

"Interesting." Deborah reached out to examine a bushy fern in detail, as if she were a botanist. Then she looked around the conservatory. "It certainly is very tropical." Her voice was matter-of-fact.

"Can't you almost see a full moon?"

She flicked him a quick, wary look. Then she

glanced around again, as if she was only now noticing the old-fashioned lanterns and the sweet scent of the bougainvillea growing in bright profusion near the fountain. "I guess," she said.

"Sure. Hanging right in that patch of sky between the two palmetto trees." His voice sounded strange, as if it weren't his. And all his senses seemed sharper than ever before. The rich scent of gardenias and the splash of water in the fountain seemed to enclose the two of them in their own private little world as Cam watched Deborah lean down to smell a hibiscus flower.

"Did you know your hair looks very gold in the light of this lantern?" He'd never seen a more beautiful color. And it wasn't fake, either. Nothing about this woman was fake. But her hair really was spectacular tonight. "I like the new style, by the way."

"Okay, that's it." Deborah stopped short on the pathway and folded her arms over her chest.

Cam blinked. "What's it?"

She gave him a severe look. "Marilyn's not here anymore, so you can turn it off right this minute."

"Off?" He felt disoriented.

"Yes. We're going to be seeing a lot of each other, so we should clear the air right now. I'm sure this kind of thing is totally automatic with you, but I don't want to deal with it."

"What kind of thing? What are you talking about?" What had he done to make Deborah so agitated? He saw anger and even, he thought, a little hurt in her eyes.

"This...this *flirty* kind of talk, the sexy glances." Deborah swallowed. "It's ridiculous and it's totally pointless, because you can't possibly be interested in me—''

"I can't?"

"—and I'm certainly not interested in you."

Cam winced. No chattiness there. The lady knew how to make her point. She also knew how to tick him off.

"Ridiculous? What do you mean by that?" She found his attention *ridiculous?*

Terrific. Just terrific.

"I mean exactly what I said. I appreciate your helping me with Marilyn, but enough's enough. The idea of our being seriously interested in each other is ridiculous, and I'm not comfortable with that much pretense."

Cam stared at her for a long moment. When he could get his voice to work, he said, "Come on. Let's go sit by the fountain."

As they walked, he took a slow, steadying breath. "Why aren't you interested in me?" He wasn't sure he wanted to know. But he had to ask.

For a moment Deborah eyed him as if he were a horse that had suddenly started talking. The splashing of the fountain seemed to fade as Cam met her gaze. The scent of roses was heavy in the air.

"I guess you find it inconceivable that a woman might not be attracted to you."

He frowned. "No, I don't. But I don't care about just any woman. I'm talking about you." Cam sat down on the brick edging around the fountain and gestured for Deborah to do the same. He was relieved when she did. "I'd appreciate it if you'd clue me in."

"You mean, you want me to catalogue all the reasons I'm not interested in you?'' She sounded incredulous.

He raised his brows. "There are that many?"

This talk was not going well.

Cam leaned forward, clasping his hands together and resting his forearms on his knees. "Maybe you could just list a few. You know, some things I can improve on."

Deborah shrugged. "You can't help being rich." As soon as she said it, she blushed and looked like she'd rather be anywhere else.

Cam frowned. Had he heard right? "Are you suggesting that my having money makes me less attractive to you?" If so, that was a first. Every other woman seemed to feel the exact opposite. It was boring and predictable how alluring his money made him. In fact, it was possible Deborah had said what she had as an original way of getting his attention.

He doubted it, though. Not only did she seem to regret saying it, but from what he knew of her so far, Deborah Clark was far too honest and proud to play games like that. She hadn't even let him buy her a dress, for God's sake.

Besides, she already had his attention. More than she wanted of it, apparently.

"Look, I really don't want to talk about it." Deborah stared down into the fountain, one slender hand clutching the brick edging.

"Is that what you meant?" Cam insisted. "My money makes me less attractive to you?" It mattered more than he wanted to think about.

"Yes, although it's not your major problem."

"Is that right?" Cam wanted to shake her. "What, pray tell, is my deadliest flaw?"

Deborah's eyes narrowed in acknowledgement of his sarcasm, but then she shrugged. "Your commitment problem."

"I do not have a commitment problem!"

A couple appeared from around the corner, gave them a startled glance and hastily retreated.

Deborah got up. "I think we should go."

"Not so fast." Cam took hold of her arm. "We haven't cleared the air." The feel of her smooth skin under his palm and fingers made his pulse accelerate.

Damn. It was inconvenient how much he wanted this woman. Inconvenient and highly annoying, especially since she apparently wanted nothing to do with him. Why was he so obsessed by a woman who thought this little of him? He really had to get Deborah Clark out of his system, and the sooner the better.

The problem was, seducing her would clearly be a bigger challenge than he'd thought.

Unless everything she'd been talking about was just that—talk. After all, surely he couldn't have imagined every single clue he'd picked up from her? She might be relatively inexperienced, but he wasn't. And every instinct he had told him Deborah was attracted to him. She might not want to be—hell, he could relate to that—but she was.

Maybe he'd better find out for sure.

"Okay, so we've established that you could never be genuinely interested in me," Cam said. "Nevertheless, as you pointed out, we'll be seeing a lot of each other over the next few weeks. And I think you'll agree that there is some amount of physical attraction between us."

Deborah frowned. "I don't see—"

"A very slight attraction." Good thing he was indoors and away from lightning bolts. Sitting next to him, her slinky dress molded to her body, Deborah was both graceful and sexy. Even as annoyed as he was with her at this moment, he wanted to kiss the pulse that beat faintly in her delicate neck. After that, he wanted to kiss her lips and then—

He cleared his throat. "If you're honest you'll admit to that."

Deborah gave him a wry smile. "Well, you *are* an attractive man, of course." Pink tinged her cheeks.

"And you're very beautiful." He heard his voice deepen. Cam dragged his gaze away from her lips and drew a steadying breath. "I think we should save ourselves the inevitable tension and the wondering about what it would be like, and just get it over with." His pulse was a loud thud in his ears.

Her brow puckered again. "Get what over with?"

"The kiss."

Deborah drew in an audible breath. "Oh, but we won't be doing that, since we're not dating. You know, since we're just..." She swallowed. "I mean, since this is a business arrangement." She was staring at Cam's mouth, though. Was it his imagination, or did she lean in slightly toward him?

"Yes, business. I know that." He also knew that if he didn't kiss her very soon, he was going to go crazy. "Trust me, this will clear everything up."

He was wrong. The second Cam's lips touched Deborah's, he realized nothing had prepared him for the feel of her lips against his. Soft, warm, welcoming. And sweet. Very sweet. Hesitant, almost girlish, as if she wasn't used to doing much kissing.

Her soft skin and the subtle, fresh scent she wore

clouded his brain, and Cam gave up trying to think. Instead he pulled her closer and gently coaxed her mouth open while his hands explored her bare back, stroking the smooth skin. He'd wanted to do that all evening, and the small shivering sigh she gave told its own story.

Her hands came up and stroked the hair at his neck, sending a jolt of pleasure through him. At the same time, her mouth firmed under his as she returned his passion in full measure. From under closed lids Cam saw a swirl of rainbow colors and bright flashes.

He groaned. He had never felt such sharp desire before, such a strong sense of urgency. They had to get out of here. Her place or his, he didn't care, but they couldn't stay here. Cam opened his eyes.

That was when he saw the photographer.

Chapter Nine

"Wow. The things you get up to when I'm not around to chaperone." Ann clicked her tongue.

Deborah clutched her robe and blinked at her friend, who stood in her doorway waving the newspaper. What was Ann talking about? She looked disgustingly bright-eyed for eight o'clock on a Monday morning, but Deborah wasn't operating at the same level. She couldn't process anything she was hearing. She hadn't even started the morning's crossword puzzle yet. She needed a cup of tea.

Or maybe ten.

She was never particularly alert first thing in the morning, but today was worse than usual. Deborah stifled a grimace. She was too old for a weekend like the one she'd just spent. Even though she and Cameron had left the party immediately after that disturbing kiss in the conservatory, it had still been late when Cameron dropped Deborah off at her apartment. Then she'd lain awake until the wee hours telling herself that even if the man was no frog, he wasn't a prince, either, or at least not her prince.

As if one sleepless night weren't enough, Deborah had spent half of Sunday night on the phone. After all, sisters were supposed to be there for each other, and Julie had needed her. So after two late nights in a row, Deborah's brain was now completely fogged up.

"Here, you'd better drink some of this." Ann handed her a large Styrofoam cup of Sweetness and Light's best breakfast blend. Deborah took a grateful sip of the tea and watched her friend settle herself in an armchair.

"How did you get in downstairs?" Strange that a small detail was the first thing her mind focused on.

Ann shrugged. "The door was open. Maybe your Cameron is already at work."

"He's not my Cameron."

Ann laughed. "Really? That's not what this photo says."

"Photo?" Deborah's gaze followed Ann's finger. "Oh, no."

The photograph was small, with no names given, but both she and Cameron were completely recognizable. And there they were, in vivid color, kissing with a passion that made her blush. Remembering that kiss all the rest of the weekend had been bad enough, but seeing it right in front of her was even worse. And knowing that a large proportion of Indianapolis was also viewing that kiss this morning over coffee and toast was the absolute worst.

How had this happened?

Deborah forced herself to breathe. Okay, so she knew how the kiss had happened. She had looked into gorgeous green eyes and seen a desire there that rooted her to the spot. A desire that forced her to acknowledge that she wanted Cameron Lyle and had to know what his kiss was like.

But how could she have lost control like that?

Deborah closed her eyes. She couldn't even blame it on alcohol. She'd had very little to drink Saturday night. Yet she had kissed Cameron with such abandon, spearing her fingers through his hair, meeting his tongue with hers, plastering her body against his. She had never in her life experienced a kiss that wild.

She had never wanted a man so badly.

Even now, the thought of that kiss made Deborah's insides quiver. She'd seen fireworks, except that now Deborah suspected what she'd actually seen behind closed lids was a photographer's flash. She'd been so caught up in Cameron's kiss that someone had snapped their photo and she hadn't even realized it.

Had Cameron? Was that why he'd suddenly gone all brisk and suggested they should call it a night? Or was his withdrawal what she'd assumed at the time, a "cold feet" reaction from a man who avoided anything that might smack of commitment?

"Val's Valentine picks," said Ann.

"What?" Deborah's head felt swimmy.

"Valerie Zynan. You know, she's the one who does the 'About Town' column. This is her Valentine's Day feature, and you two not only appear in her 'Most Romantic Moments' photo collection, as you've seen, but you also made it into her gossip column."

"Terrific," Deborah muttered.

"Here, I'll read you the paragraph about you two. That'll wake you up." Ann had an unholy gleam in her eye as she reached for the newspaper.

Deborah evaded her. "Thank you very much, but I'll read it myself." She sank down onto the couch.

Her friend was quickly losing the brownie points she'd won for bringing tea.

The paragraph only had six lines, but they were deadly. Deborah read them and wanted to scream.

She'd kill him.

This was worse than she could have guessed. The reporter practically had them engaged, and it could only be Cameron who'd given her the false information. Thanks to his machinations, not to mention his high-profile lifestyle, the two of them would probably be a hot topic for days, if not weeks. And once they stopped attending events together, Deborah would get to be dumped all over again, even if fictiously.

It shouldn't matter to her what people thought. And, up to a point, it didn't. But nobody liked to be pitied, and she'd already been through that only a couple of months ago when Mark broke up with her. It was too fresh in her mind.

As cheerful as she'd been about her broken engagement, everyone had still been solicitous and careful of her, sure that she must be brokenhearted somewhere beneath her breeziness. She hadn't liked the reflection of herself that she saw in their eyes. It reminded her too much of that other Deborah, the young girl whose classmates had felt sorry for her because everyone knew her father had abandoned her.

She would never allow herself to feel like that, or to be pitied like that, again.

"I had no idea you've been dating for weeks." Ann helped herself to orange juice from the fridge. Her voice held accusation and a tinge of hurt.

"That's because we haven't been."

Ann gave her a long stare. "Okay, so she's wrong

about the past history stuff. But you're obviously dating now, and you never breathed a word to me.''

''We are *not* dating.'' Deborah met her friend's gaze. ''I know that photo makes it look like we are, but that was only a test kiss, not anything...'' She waved a hand. ''Never mind. It just wasn't important, that's all.'' Except that she'd learned to never again let Cameron Lyle kiss her. It was too dangerous.

What a pity she hadn't learned that lesson just a little bit sooner.

WHEN HIS OFFICE DOOR flew open, Cam looked up from his desk. ''Good morning.''

''As a matter of fact, it isn't,'' Deborah informed him. She stalked into his office and slapped a newspaper down in front of him. ''As you could probably guess.''

Cam eyed her. Whatever had set Deborah off, it wasn't anything small. She looked more steamed than he'd ever seen her, even madder than when he'd bought her the dress. Judging by how tousled her hair was, she'd thrown on her blue sweater and leggings and come straight down without showering or even combing her hair.

She looked good. In fact, she looked sexy. The sight of Deborah always gave him a jolt of energy, but today he was getting even more voltage than usual. That was undoubtedly because she was mad, but still, one simple glance at her had his body reacting in a disturbing, and by now familiar, way. If he thought any more about how Deborah was probably still warm from her bed, he would lose it.

Just the way he'd nearly lost it Saturday night. One kiss from her, and he'd been desperate to make love to her. If he hadn't been brought sharply back to earth by the sight of that photographer, he'd have carried Deborah off to do exactly that, and he wouldn't have been fussy about the place, either.

Seducing Deborah wasn't supposed to be like this. *He* wasn't like this.

He didn't lose control. That wasn't something he did. Period. He'd desired a lot of women in his lifetime, but he'd never kissed one and felt himself start to shake. He'd never been consumed by a need to experience one particular woman's touch.

And he'd never had even a suspicion that making love with a woman would change him forever.

The only possible strategy was to beat a hasty retreat, and that was exactly what he'd done Saturday night. He'd spent Sunday calling himself ten kinds of a fool for letting his imagination run away with him. No woman could possibly have that strong an effect on him. He had nothing to worry about.

Except maybe his bodily safety. Because right now, Deborah was madder than hell. Good thing Barb wasn't in yet. He wouldn't want her to get caught in the cross fire.

Plus, he could do without any more teasing from his assistant.

"What I don't get is how you did it," Deborah said, looking like she couldn't decide whether to hit him or strangle him.

"Did what? What are you talking about?"

She stabbed a finger at the newspaper she'd thrown down on his desk. "Take a look at that."

It was an excellent photo. Clear, close-up and well composed. And it was unmistakably Deborah and himself, locked in a kiss that made him hot all over again just looking at it.

Cam cleared his throat. "Good photo." He looked up and met her accusing stare. "What, you think I had something to do with it?"

Her eyes narrowed. "Did you or did you not know that photographer was there?"

Remembering his sighting of the cameraman through the trees, Cam hesitated.

Deborah nodded, her face set. "That's what I thought."

Her expression stung. What kind of unchivalrous jerk did she think he was? "No, it is *not* what you thought. I only saw him after the fact, at which point I hustled you out of the hotel as fast as I could."

"Uh-huh. And I suppose you had nothing to do with telling what's-her-name, that sleaze reporter, that we've been dating for weeks and might be serious about each other?"

"What sleaze reporter?" He frowned. "I don't see any of that here. We aren't even identified."

"No, that info is in her gossip column." Deborah stared at him, and for the first time since she'd stormed into his office, she looked something less than homicidal. But she still looked upset, and Cam felt his own irritation fade.

"I'm sorry," he said. "I didn't give out any information, but I should have anticipated the photographer problem, because they always take pictures at benefits like Saturday night's. It's part of the publicity angle for the charity, and everyone who goes tacitly agrees to be photographed. But I wasn't thinking about that when I kissed you."

Cam grimaced. Of course not. The only thing he'd

been able to think about was having Deborah in his arms. In fact, even if he'd remembered about photographers, he had no faith he'd have been able to stop himself from kissing her.

Like he wanted to do right now.

"It'll all blow over," Cam assured her. "Give it a week or two, and no one's going to remember any of this. Most people don't take gossip column stuff all that seriously." He shrugged. "Of course, it's hard not to when you're the subject, but the best strategy is to say nothing and wait for them to start talking about somebody else."

"Uh-huh. Well, you would know, wouldn't you?" she muttered. She still stood in front of his desk, her gaze locked on his.

"That's right." He studied her. "You know, it seems to me you're a lot less laid-back these days than you used to be. You need to reduce your stress level. You should watch your caffeine intake."

For a long moment Deborah stared at him. Then she laughed. A little wildly, but it was definitely a laugh. "Touché. And I am watching it. In about two minutes I'm going to Sweetness and Light to eat a mocha brownie and watch my caffeine intake go straight through the roof."

"Sounds like fun." Cam grinned. He liked a woman who could laugh at herself. She had small crinkles at the corners of her eyes. He wanted to kiss those crinkles. But if he did, he wouldn't stop there. He'd have to kiss her soft, full lips, too. He'd have to run his hands through her glorious, tousled golden hair. And then he'd want to touch her everywhere—

The outer office door opened and shut, signaling Barb's arrival, and they both gave a start. Cam knew why he jumped, but he found Deborah's reaction interesting.

Maybe he wasn't the only one who'd been thinking about kissing.

TWO HOURS LATER Deborah hung up the phone and knew she had to go talk to Cameron.

Drat.

She wasn't nervous, she told herself as she headed down the stairs. She just felt a bit defensive and more than a little sheepish.

He stood in the hallway at the foot of the staircase, and just like that she was tongue-tied. Why was the man always bigger than she remembered? It was both annoying and strange, since she wasn't exactly tiny herself. Cameron Lyle was only four or five inches taller than her, so why did he seem to tower over her?

Halfway down the stairs, Deborah stopped. "Look, I just wanted to say—"

"Wait a minute." Cameron took the stairs three at a time, passing her and continuing on up to the top.

"Where are you going?" Deborah hurried up after him. What an aggravating man. She would much rather have apologized from her distance, not to mention her greater height, on the staircase, with him down below. Now he stood outside her door, making the walls of the hallway seem to close in on her.

"Let's talk up here. No point in getting any more gossip started, is there?" Cameron gave her a challenging smile as he opened her door.

"That's what I wanted to talk to you about." Deborah followed him inside, stifling her irritation at his presumption in opening her door. "I just got a call from Marilyn, apologizing for talking about us to someone she had no idea was a reporter. Of course, Marilyn got most of her information from me. So, indirectly at least, the *reliable source* turns out to be myself. How's that for irony?'' She grimaced. ''I apologize for accusing you, and also for getting us into that gossip column.''

Cameron sat down on her couch. ''I'll forgive you. For a price.''

Deborah shot him a wary look.

''Do you have any of those gingersnaps left?''

She blinked at him, and he chuckled. ''Did you think I was going to demand something more interesting?'' His eyes held a glint.

She fought a blush. ''With you, who knows?''

She went to look for the cookies, glad of an excuse to disappear into the kitchen. His gracious acceptance of her apology surprised her. In her experience, this man had a low tolerance for inconvenience. Becoming the subject of gossip around town had to be more of an inconvenience than a feline intruder or an overflowing mailbox.

On the other hand, as she had only just realized again, Cameron Lyle was used to people gossiping about him. Obviously it wasn't a big deal.

When she went back into the living room and handed him the box of gingersnaps, Cameron gave her a strange look.

''What's the matter?'' Deborah asked.

He held out the box. ''Aren't you going to have any?''

She shook her head. ''It's almost lunchtime.''

Cameron looked at his watch. ''I guess so. Does that mean I don't get tea this time?'' Without waiting for a response, he chose a cookie and crunched into it.

Deborah looked at him in surprise. "You want tea?"

"No, I don't. I'm a coffee person." He munched some more. "As you may have noticed."

In spite of herself, she smiled. "You're impossible."

"I know. That's part of my charm, though, don't you think?" He looked up at her, the boyish tilt to his mouth at odds with the very male, very aware look in his eyes. It was the same look he'd given her downstairs when she'd burst into his office. But at least then she'd had her anger to keep her occupied.

Now it was an effort to stay relaxed.

"I'll get back to you on that," Deborah said dryly.

Cameron had made himself completely at home on her couch. He leaned against the cushions at one end, his legs sprawled across half of the couch. He finished his second cookie and handed the box back to her as he looked around the room. "Where's Libby?"

"Probably sleeping on my bed."

He nodded. "Are you still upset?"

His sudden change of topic caught her off guard, which might have been on purpose. Deborah tried to read the expression in Cameron's vivid green eyes and failed. Finally she shrugged. "I'm not exactly happy about it, but the gossip column is all my own fault, isn't it? And chances are, people around here won't believe it, anyway."

"What do you mean?" He beckoned her over to the couch.

Deborah sat next to him. "It's obvious. Everybody

knows you choose stylish, beautiful women to get involved with.''

He frowned. ''So? You're a beautiful woman.''

She laughed.

He gave her a long look. ''You don't believe me?''

Deborah shrugged. There was no point in being
rude. But this man was used to women who not only
had spectacular raw material to work with, but also
were a lot more interested in fashionable clothes, hair
and makeup than she ever wanted to be. Not to mention women who had the money to indulge those interests.

Cameron gave a low whistle. ''Wow. This ex-
fiancé of yours must have really done a number on
you.''

''No, he didn't. As a matter of fact, I'm grateful to
him for breaking it off.'' Deborah stifled a wince.
Why had she told him that? It was true, but probably
not very believable. There were plenty of other truths
she could have told him that would be more credible.
And equally not his business. She didn't owe him any
explanations. Why did this man bring out every defensive impulse in her?

''Really?'' He looked a lot more interested than
Deborah would ever have imagined he could be, at
least in anything concerning her.

Deborah gave him a pointed glance. ''Yes, really.''

''Why are you grateful?'' Cameron asked.

Her eyes narrowed.

''I'm just trying to make sure there aren't any broken hearts around here.'' His gaze was searching, intent. Warm, even. He looked concerned.

Right, and he probably cried buckets every time he
dumped a woman, too.

"No broken hearts," Deborah told him. "Now why don't we talk about something that's actually your business?"

He raised a brow. "Ouch."

She grimaced. What was wrong with her? She wasn't usually rude. The magnetic and nerve-wracking Cameron Lyle was having a disastrous effect on her personality.

Of course, this morning's events hadn't helped, either.

Cameron sent her an exaggeratedly patient look. "You could be a little friendlier since we're going out together."

"We're *not* going out." Heaven forbid. A few months of that kind of involvement with him and who knew what personality disasters would befall her? She could make Lizzie Borden look well-adjusted.

"Of course we're not," he agreed. "It was a figure of speech. Still, we can't stay complete strangers, can we?"

"Why not?" Deborah muttered. It was the smart thing to do.

"Excuse me?"

She sighed. Okay, so they already knew too much about each other to be total strangers. Still, it was illogical—and possibly dangerous—to provide any more information to a man who was just as wrong for her as he was attractive to her.

"Never mind." Deborah gave him an innocent smile. "You know, if you want to talk about broken hearts, we could start by discussing all the ones you've scattered around town. Then we could move on to analyze why your relationships don't last."

There. That ought to do it.

He frowned. "Is this where you tell me, for approximately the thousandth time, that I'm commitment phobic?"

"No, it's where I tell you that part of your problem is you don't see the women you date as people."

Cameron raised his eyes to the ceiling. "That's ridiculous. Of course they're people. What else would they be?"

Thoughtfully Deborah regarded the man who sat so nonchalantly next to her on the couch. He was intelligent, funny and generous, she had discovered that much over the last couple of weeks. He was way more attractive than she wanted to admit. And in spite of what she'd thought when she first met him, Cameron could be quite a charmer, in an unexpectedly genuine kind of way.

Yet he was determined to believe that passion was the most to be hoped for in a relationship. He was way too cynical. And just stubborn enough to refuse to recognize love even if it hit him over the head.

What a waste.

"Okay, I'll bite. What makes you think I don't see women as people?" Cameron asked. His tone was light, almost flippant, but his eyes told her he really wanted to know.

Deborah shrugged. "I can only speak for what I've noticed, and it's hard to explain. But there's something so...*practiced* about those sexy glances and flirtatious little touches you give me sometimes. It's as if all you're seeing when you look at me is a female, any female. As if you're thinking, *Me Tarzan, you Jane,* you know? It makes everything seem impersonal. Of course, I realize ours isn't a typical situation, since you're not romantically interested in me," she added hastily.

For a few seconds he said nothing, simply sat there looking incredulous. "My kiss gave you the impression I'm not interested in you?" Cameron's voice rose in pitch. He shook his head. "God, I must really be slipping."

All at once, with only those few words, she was back in the conservatory, in his arms. Feeling the heat of his hands on her bare back, the passion in his lips so fierce on hers.

Deborah blushed. Unable to meet his gaze, she bent her head. "You're not slipping. But that was a fluke," she muttered. "You know, romantic flowers, a fountain. We both got carried away."

"I see. A fluke. It could never happen again, right?"

Deborah heard the challenge in his voice and lifted her head as warning bells went off.

Oh, no. He was going to kiss her. She could read it in his eyes, feel it in the stillness of him.

Yes, in about two seconds he was going to kiss her. And she shouldn't let him. She should be drawing back right this instant, putting a mile or so between them.

Deborah stared at him, hypnotized by the desire she saw in his eyes. She forced herself to look away from his eyes, only to find her attention caught and held by his strong jaw. She wanted to smooth it with her fingers. She wanted to touch his mouth, too, so firm and well shaped.

Heaven help her, she wanted to kiss him more than anything.

Cameron's mouth covered hers, and she closed her

eyes. He tasted like ginger, warm and fragrant. The touch of his lips was light and exploratory at first, but then it deepened into a pressure which demanded, and got, a response.

Deborah opened her mouth to his. She was drowning in sensation. She clutched him around the neck. His hair waved just above his collar, and the ends of it were soft against her fingertips. She felt as shell-shocked as she had the last time he'd kissed her, and she leaned against his chest, feeling the strength there, the answering thud of his heart. When his tongue probed the inner corners of her mouth, she sent her own tongue to meet it, to explore more deeply the taste of him.

This was crazy. Why couldn't she resist this man? He was all wrong for her. He was disaster waiting to happen. For weeks she'd been telling herself she wasn't going to have anything to do with Cameron Lyle, but she'd been fighting a losing battle.

There was nothing left to do but give in.

Deborah let him push her gently back against the couch. His hand found her breast, exploring the shape of it through her clingy green top. With his fingertip he rubbed her nipple, and she shivered. Deborah slipped one of his shirt buttons free and caressed his chest, sending a small shudder through him. His mouth came down on hers again, and she moaned.

Cameron's head lifted. He was breathing hard as he eased away from her. "Look me straight in the eye and tell me I'm not interested in you," he said in a hoarse whisper. She saw him swallow in a convulsive movement. "Then tell me you're not interested in me."

Deborah closed her eyes. She lowered her head until her chin rested on her upper chest. How could she have let herself get so carried away?

Again.

Hadn't she learned anything at all the first time he'd kissed her? This man was dangerous. Or, to be more accurate and more honest, the passion he aroused in her was dangerous. With one touch, he made her feel completely out of control.

"Can you do that?" Cameron grasped her chin and turned her face toward him until her eyes were only inches from his blazing green ones. His voice was low, urgent. "If you can look straight at me and tell me it was all a mistake, that I'm the only one who feels this...this..." He swallowed again. "If you can tell me that, then we'll forget all about any kind of romance between us, and I'll leave you alone."

Deborah stared at him. She wished she could tell him that. She wanted to so badly her throat hurt.

But she couldn't. Because it would be a lie, and he knew it.

"Exactly," Cameron whispered.

Her phone rang, and Deborah almost shrieked with relief when it turned out to be a business call and Cameron headed for the door.

She took a long, shaky breath. Sooner or later she would have to tell him that it really didn't matter if they were attracted to each other. The bottom line was that she had no intention of getting sexually involved with him. She refused to be just another throwaway girlfriend. It was a lot safer staying as they were, friends who happened to be attracted to each other.

She would explain all of that—well, most of it— later. Just because *later* turned out to be much better

than *sooner* didn't mean she wasn't going to do it.
She was. She would sit him down and lay it all on
the line.

Later.

Chapter Ten

"Have you seen Deborah?"

Cam looked up. Barb stood in his doorway, a strange look on her face.

"No," he said. "I haven't seen her since yesterday."

"Neither have I. Which is really strange."

Lucky was the word Cam would have chosen. Not that he didn't want to see Deborah, because he did.

That was the problem.

He'd cut back on caffeine with no trouble at all, but apparently he had next to no willpower where one Deborah Clark was concerned. The fact that she popped in and out of his office with no advance warning didn't help, either.

"Why is it strange?" Cam asked, since Barb was still standing there, squinting at him through her reading glasses and looking as if she expected some kind of response.

"Well, it's Tuesday."

He gave her what he knew had to be a blank look. What did Tuesday have to do with anything?

"It's her volunteer day at Kids First." His assistant took her glasses off and perched them on her gray head. "Deborah spends the morning helping out in the day-care center, but she's usually back shortly after eleven—the kids eat lunch early, you know—and then she and I have tea and she tells me what funny things the toddlers got up to."

"I see." Actually, he didn't. He'd never have pictured Deborah doing volunteer work. Cam frowned. "Well, she's probably just running late."

"I guess." Barb sounded unconvinced.

He looked at her. "You're thinking she'd have phoned if that were the case?"

"Yes, I am. Deborah's very reliable."

True. Not very long ago, he'd have guessed exactly the opposite. But in spite of her breezy, flippant tendencies, Deborah did what she said she was going to do.

Cam thought for a moment. "Do you know what time she goes to this day care?"

"I think around eight."

"Well, I was here by then, and I never heard her come down." Cam didn't want to think about how early he'd gotten to work. Or why he'd finally given up trying to get any more sleep.

Soft curves. Sweet lips. Slender hands that drove him wild.

Brilliant blue eyes filled with dismay.

He and Barb looked at each other. "Okay, let's go up there," Cam suggested.

Their knock brought no response. The door was locked. Cam knocked again, louder, and this time they heard an insistent meowing, followed by a thump.

"That was too big a thump to be Libby," Barb said. Alarm filled her hazel eyes. "We've got to get in there.'' She tried the knob again. "Do you have a key?''

"No.'' Cam examined the door. He was too worried about Deborah to care about correcting Barb's assumption that the two of them were sexually involved. It was a moot point, anyway, since he planned to get involved with Deborah in the very near future. Furthermore, he suspected his assistant, who had seen yesterday's paper, wouldn't believe any denials.

A groan sounded inside the apartment.

Cam drew in a breath.

"Oh, it sounds like she's hurt,'' Barb wailed. "What are we going to do?''

"I'm going to pick this lock, which is fortunately pathetic.''

A few moments later, they were inside.

Where was Deborah?

Cam headed for a doorway and almost collided with her. He grasped Deborah's shoulders to steady her and was shocked at how hot her skin felt under her thin robe.

"Food,'' she muttered, teeth chattering. She stared at him with glazed eyes that didn't seem to see him. Her hair fell in limp strands to her shoulders. A sheen of sweat covered her ghostly pale face.

"Flu,'' Barb announced behind him.

"Come on, Deborah, you need to get back in bed.'' Cam felt sudden fear. He'd never seen anyone look this sick from the flu. Could it be something else? Could she die from this, whatever it was?

Deborah shook her head. "Food. Poor Libby.'' She shivered violently.

"I'll feed her, dear,'' Barb said in reassuring tones.

''Don't worry about Libby. She'll be fine. You just get back into bed. Come on, now, let Cam help you.''

It must have been her motherly voice that did the trick. Deborah let him help her over to the bed.

''I'm also going to find some soup to heat up for her.'' Barb vanished.

Cam studied Deborah, who sat obediently on her bed, looking totally out of it. He would have to get his doctor over here, because there was no point in taking chances with her health. Meanwhile, he'd better get her under the covers. Cam eased off her threadbare excuse for a robe and got his first surprise.

She wore nothing but panties underneath. Skimpy fuchsia bikini panties.

Cam closed his eyes. Then he drew in a breath and rooted around in her dresser until he found a long T-shirt. Keeping his gaze resolutely on her face, he dressed her and then tucked her under the covers.

The woman was sick. Very sick. This was no time to be thinking about what she was or wasn't wearing. If she knew what was going on, Deborah would be horrified and probably resentful that he was here. He ought to get Barb to take over.

On the other hand, his assistant had more than enough demands on her time. Her husband wasn't strong, and she was still getting caught up with her work after her own bout with the flu. She needed her rest, and since someone would have to stay with Deborah tonight, he was the logical choice, at least until they could get ahold of Deborah's friend Ann.

''How's our patient?'' Barb appeared in the doorway, holding a steaming mug. ''Chicken noodle soup.''

''You found the cat food?''

"Yes. Libby's almost finished it already, poor thing. Way past her feeding time." Barb shook her head. "I hate to think of Deborah lying here all this time and us having no idea."

Cam winced. "We'd still have no idea if you hadn't gotten worried. Are you sure this is the flu?"

"Looks like it to me. Fever, sweats. She probably aches everywhere. It's a respiratory flu, not a stomach flu, but it's a doozy. I could barely get out of bed for days. And when the cough set in, I was an even more unhappy camper." Barb frowned. "She'll need someone with her. Are you going to stay?"

"Yes." Cam had no more doubts about that. The simple truth was, he didn't trust anyone else to be vigilant enough. If Deborah complained once she was better, if she wanted someone like her friend Ann to stay with her instead, then he would leave. But he was here now, and he would take good care of her.

"I'm going to get my doctor over here," Cam said. "Just to be sure she doesn't have something worse. We might as well cover all the bases."

Barb nodded. Cam thought a smile lit her eyes, but he didn't have time to think any more about it.

He had a patient to take care of.

DEBORAH FROWNED at the voices in her head. Had she left the radio on? The DJs were talking way too loudly, and her head hurt. Come to think of it, her whole body hurt, and her throat felt practically raw.

She started to get up to turn off the radio, but hands pushed her back and then she felt something cold on her chest. More words floated around the room, words like *flu* and *rest* and *fine,* but then someone must have turned the radio off, because blissful silence filled her bedroom. Deborah settled her head into her pillow with a sigh of relief.

CAM GOT BACK from his whirlwind grocery trip shortly before five o'clock, just in time to relieve Barb and let her get home.

"That was fast." When he'd finished bringing up all the bags, she smiled at him, her brows arched. "I'll know who to call next time I need masses of groceries in less than a half hour."

"I'm sure your kitchen is much better stocked than Deborah's." Cam shook his head. "Pathetic."

"I notice she has a good stash of frozen dinners."

He snorted, and Barb laughed.

After she'd left, Cam finished stowing away the groceries and started fixing a simple stew. Deborah probably wouldn't be in any shape to eat dinner, but his stomach was reminding him he'd skipped lunch. And he had no intention of eating any wimpy frozen dinners.

Eventually he would have to go get his sleeping bag and blanket from the emergency winter kit he kept in the trunk of his car. The floor wouldn't be the warmest place to sleep, but the couch was too short and the way she was thrashing around, Deborah needed her queen-size bed to herself.

Besides, his fantasies about sharing that bed with her did not involve either of them being prostrate with the flu.

Now that Dr. Samuelson had reassured him, Cam could feel the adrenaline from his anxiety begin to fade and weariness take over. But the familiar motions of making the stew were comforting.

Libby padded over and twined herself around his

ankles. Cam offered her a small piece of cooked chicken breast and felt her sandpaper tongue swipe across his fingers. "Looks like it's just you and me, kitty," he said, and smiled when the cat gave a small meow in response.

DEBORAH ROUSED HERSELF enough to drink from the glass, grateful for the coolness of the water sliding down her throat and also grateful for the hands that held the glass and supported her head. She caught a whiff of citrus, a scent so familiar her heart almost stopped.

"*Dad.*" She caught her breath on a sigh.

He'd come. He knew she was sick and he was here to take care of her. Joy filled her, expanding in her chest until it hurt. Her dad had come back and now they would go fishing again and play cards for hours. He would tweak her ponytail, laugh and tell her they were two of a kind, his voice ringing with pride.

"Deborah?"

She focused then and saw the lime wedges bobbing in the water. She heard the male voice and knew that although it was a familiar one, it was not her dad's. Her dad had left them and was never coming back.

And because it had been so vivid, so *real,* her sorrow, grief and anger all crowded in on her at once, and Deborah sobbed.

Arms came around her, enfolded her. She accepted a shoulder, gentle pats on her back and soft murmurs of comfort as she cried it all out.

Then she slept.

CAM OPENED his eyes to darkness, not sure what had woken him up. He was a little cold, true, but mostly he thought he'd heard something. It might have been Deborah, but it could also have been the creak of old floorboards as he rolled over, trying to get comfortable in his sleeping bag on the thin area rug. Or it could have been the creaky hum of the ancient refrigerator, shuddering out its last gasps in the kitchen.

And there was always Libby, snoring away at the foot of Deborah's bed. How could a sleeping cat be that loud? Then again, how could a fully clawed cat be unable to climb trees?

Libby the Wonder Cat.

Cam extricated himself from his sleeping bag and stood up. He would just feel Deborah's forehead and see what her temperature was like. He picked his way carefully through the dimness, grateful for the faint glow of streetlamps through Deborah's miniblinds. It wasn't as if he had far to go, since he was sleeping mere feet from her bed. But he had to go around it, since she apparently slept on the right side.

He wasn't even going to think about the other side of that bed.

Her forehead felt cool and free of perspiration, which was a relief since he'd already changed her sheets once and he'd only found one spare set in the linen closet. The ones she was sleeping on now were a bright floral, so like Deborah that he'd smiled as he put them on the bed.

Her whole bedroom was like her, in fact. She had sunny yellow curtains, a turquoise bedspread and several large, colorful floral prints on the walls.

And she wore fuchsia panties.

Cam grimaced. He couldn't afford to think about those for at least a week. According to Dr. Samuelson, he had three days of nursing duty ahead of him.

Three days during which he'd be in close and intimate contact with Deborah. Thoughts like the one he'd just had weren't going to help. After those three days, she would still be recuperating. Judging by Barb's recovery rate, it might be well over a week before he and Deborah could continue what they'd started on her couch, and that was assuming he managed to convince her that having an affair was the best thing that could happen to both of them.

He wished he didn't keep seeing large blue eyes filled with dismay.

Cam watched Deborah sleep for a while, but she seemed peaceful, so it must not have been her he'd heard. Considering how upset she'd been yesterday evening, he'd half expected more of the same during the night. He'd dreaded it, too, since he felt completely inadequate to comfort her.

She'd muttered something about her father leaving, but maybe Cam should find out where he was and if he could come. After all, Deborah might only have the flu, but it was a vicious strain, and her recovery would be slower if something was bothering her.

With only one wistful glance at the warm—and empty—left side of Deborah's bed, Cam settled back into his sleeping bag and closed his eyes.

DEBORAH WOKE to find the morning sunshine doing its best to sneak through her blinds. She yawned. Her throat still hurt and her body ached, but her various aches and pains were more bearable this morning. She stretched cautiously. Then she frowned. When had she put this T-shirt on? She had no memory of doing that.

Her mind suddenly flooded with a bunch of jumbled, distorted images. A hand on her water glass, an arm around her. Heat, lots of heat. And voices, both male and female.

Dreams?

Deborah sat straight up in bed, ignoring her muscles' protests. What was going on?

A faint noise caught her attention. It was unidentifiable, but it came from the opposite side of her room. Deborah leaned across her bed.

And saw Cameron lying on her bedroom floor, sound asleep in a sleeping bag.

She drew in a sharp breath. What was he doing here? The images in her mind shifted like colors in a kaleidoscope, and she realized it was his voice she'd heard, his arms she'd felt around her. Cameron had been here all night? Had held her in his arms? Made love to her?

Deborah's cheeks burned.

No. That was impossible. If they'd spent the night making love, she wouldn't feel this awful and Cameron wouldn't be sleeping on the floor. No, she was sick, that much was clear. She must have caught the flu that was going around. And Cameron had obviously gotten stuck taking care of her.

Deborah stared at his face. Long lashes, far thicker than she'd realized, lay in dark crescents on his cheeks. His hair was tousled, his formidable jaw shadowed with stubble. She suppressed a smile. Even sleep couldn't make that jaw of his anything but stubborn-looking. And gorgeous, just like the rest of his chiseled features. His body was unforgettable, too, what little she'd seen of it.

She couldn't see any more details this morning, either, since he was bundled up so thoroughly in his sleeping bag. She shouldn't be staring at him while he slept, but she couldn't seem to help herself. Besides, he must have looked at her at least once. Stifling her guilt, Deborah returned her gaze to his face.

And found his eyes open, looking straight into hers. Her heart skipped a beat. "Hi." She struggled against a blush, without any success. If she was lucky, he would think it was her fever coming back. She felt shaky enough she could almost convince herself.

"Good morning." His voice was husky, intimate sounding. A little untamed, like his jaw. It was a voice whose owner was well aware that they were both in bed, even if those beds weren't the same. It was a voice that conjured up a whole lot of images, none of them safe.

Why couldn't Cameron Lyle be slack-jawed and grizzled first thing in the morning?

"How do you feel?" He got up, and she could see he wore a navy turtleneck and sweats. Baggy as they were, they did nothing to hide the lean strength of the body beneath them.

"I'm fine," Deborah said hurriedly. She saw his disbelieving smile and flushed. Darn it, why had she said that? Even an idiot wouldn't believe her, and he was no idiot. She didn't even want to think about what she looked like. Probably something the cat dragged in.

The cat. *Libby.*

Deborah drew in a breath at the sudden memory. Libby was hungry, and Deborah had fallen out of bed trying to get to the kitchen. She couldn't remember what happened after that, but she had a feeling she'd never gotten the cat food.

"Where's Libby? I need to feed her." Deborah got

out of bed, felt the room tilt, and promptly sat back down. She felt dizzy, light-headed and faintly nauseated. Even worse, she had the niggling feeling she was forgetting something, an important detail.

"Steady, there." Cameron's voice held concern. "I've already fed Libby. She's fine. Unlike you." He handed her the robe she kept on a chair next to the bed. "You, my dear, independent Deborah, have the flu."

She grimaced. "Okay, so I've been better. Thank you for baby-sitting me, although I have no idea how you got here."

If only her robe were about ten times thicker. Then maybe she'd feel less weird about sitting here on her bed with Cameron only inches away. Still, at least her legs were now covered. Maybe that was the best she could hope for.

"Barb was worried, so we came up and happened to get here just in time to hear a thump," Cameron said.

Barb. Tuesday tea.

Deborah frowned. "You'll have to run that by me again in a minute. Right now I have to call Kids First, tell them I'm not going to make it."

He looked confused. "You volunteer on Wednesdays, too?"

"No, only Tuesdays." Deborah saw his expression and drew in a sharp breath. "You mean today is…?" She couldn't finish. The thought was too horrible.

"Wednesday." Cameron was nodding. "You slept all of yesterday."

She'd lost an entire day. That meant twenty-four hours unaccounted for, except for a few vague, dreamlike impressions. Deborah swallowed. Good thing she was sitting down. As it was, her heart was racing, and small wonder. Even a determined hang-loose-and-never-worry person like herself could be excused for finding news like that disconcerting.

But the loss of a day wasn't what bothered her the most. No, what really bugged her was the knowledge that Cameron had seen her at her most vulnerable. Even though he'd probably only been here overnight, it was a virtual certainty that he now knew a lot more intimate details about her than she knew about him.

At least she didn't have to worry that he'd heard feverish ramblings of undying love. After all, with a history like hers, she wasn't foolish enough to fall in love with a man who was the ultimate leaver.

Still, she was strongly attracted to Cameron Lyle, and apparently that attraction was mutual. She didn't know what she was going to do about it. And here he was, on her home turf.

Deborah looked down at herself and then at her bed. Had Cameron dressed her in this T-shirt? Had he changed her sheets and helped her to the bathroom?

"Barb's been here off and on, helping me out," said Cameron, as if he knew exactly what was going through her mind.

Deborah looked at him. His green eyes were both shrewd and sympathetic. Relief flooded through her. Yes, she remembered a female voice. Naturally, Barb would have been the one who helped her with the more personal tasks.

"I brought you something," he said, and handed her a box.

It bore the name of Stella's shop in distinctive silver lettering. Deborah eyed it warily.

"Don't worry, it's not a dress." His voice carried the hint of a smile. "Open it."

Inside she found a robe. A beautiful ivory robe in plush, soft cotton. Elegantly plain, but with quality woven in every stitch. It was the finest nightwear she'd ever owned, and she knew it had to have been expensive. Deborah smoothed down the collar, wanting to accept it and knowing she shouldn't.

She looked up.

"I'm not going to take it back," Cameron said.

She cracked a smile. "Not even for one of your emergency back-up girlfriends?"

He tossed a pillow at her.

"Thank you," she said quietly.

"You're welcome. Now how about some breakfast?" Cameron suggested, and Deborah was surprised to find that she was hungry.

She was even more surprised at the omelet and toast he presented her with a short time later. Stuffed with onions, green pepper and cheddar cheese, the omelet was better than many she'd eaten in restaurants. Better presented, too, although a parsley garnish seemed strangely formal when, at Cameron's insistence, she was eating in bed. At least she'd managed to get dressed. Cameron sat drinking a glass of orange juice on a chair he'd borrowed from the kitchen.

"This is incredible. How did you learn to cook?" She'd always figured someone as rich as Cameron had servants to cook for him. Moreover, he'd been born into a wealthy family, so why would he ever have learned that skill?

"From our housekeeper." He smiled. "Sally said if I was going to spend so much time in the kitchen, I might as well learn to do something useful."

"Somehow I can't see you hanging out in the kitchen."

He shrugged. "Sally was always there and always happy to see me."

Meaning his parents hadn't been? Cameron was an only child, she remembered that much. It seemed like a lousy deal. She didn't want to even imagine growing up without her sister.

"Where is Sally now?" Deborah savored another bite of egg.

He smiled. "She's retired, but she works part-time for me."

"What about your parents? You said they're divorced." Still, people fought hard to keep good staff.

"Divorced, yes—three times, each—and living in Chicago." He chuckled. "They see a lot more of each other now than they did when they were married. They've even turned into human beings."

Deborah hesitated. "And before that they weren't?" she asked finally, unable to stop herself.

"Not that I remember. Most of the time they weren't around, and when they were, they fought bitterly, usually over me." He shook his head. "That was one custody battle I'll bet the judge didn't forget very soon."

It was obvious Cameron himself would never forget it. He was smiling, but she could see the remnants of childhood pain in his eyes.

"How old were you?" Deborah asked.

"Ten."

She winced.

"Speaking of parents," Cameron said, "maybe you should get in touch with yours." It sounded like a casual suggestion, but she could sense him watching her.

"Why? Is there something I should know about this flu?" Deborah tried to sound amused but wasn't sure she pulled it off. Did he think she was a complete baby? "Barb recovered just fine."

"It's got nothing to do with the flu," Cameron said. "I just get the impression you miss your father."

Deborah stared at him, and then she knew. It hadn't all been a dream. Only the part about her dad. The rest, including the arms holding her, had been Cameron.

She cleared her throat. "Yeah, well, I do miss him. But there's nothing I can do about that, because he's dead."

Surprise filled Cameron's eyes. For a long moment he just looked at her. "I see. So that's what you meant about him leaving."

Deborah almost let him believe that. It would have been easier for her. Nothing to relive, no pain to rake over. No privacy sacrificed.

But she had never glossed over the facts, except to strangers. And whatever else he might be, Cameron wasn't a stranger.

"No," she said. "That's not what I meant. My father left us when I was thirteen. He was killed by a drunk driver four days later."

Cameron was silent for so long she almost thought he hadn't heard her. Finally he asked, "Is that why you don't have his picture anywhere?"

She frowned. "That has nothing to do with it."

"I see. How did your mom handle his leaving?"

"She was worried. My mother was convinced he was clinically depressed, and she wanted him to get help." Deborah sighed. "Mom's positive Dad would have come back if he'd lived."

"You don't agree?"

"I have no way of knowing. None of us do." Her throat tightened up, so she stopped talking and shrugged instead.

"I'm sorry," Cameron said.

Deborah met his gaze for one long, silent moment. Then she had to look away. "So am I, but that's life, you know?" She blinked. "And to answer your original question, I don't think I'm sick enough to bother my mom down in Florida. Or to keep you from your work, for that matter." She smiled at him. "Thanks for a really good breakfast."

Cameron raised a brow. "Thanks and goodbye?"

She flushed. "I didn't mean it that way. I appreciate everything you've done, but I don't want you getting way behind because of me. I can call Ann and get her to look in on her way home."

He shook his head. "Ann has the flu, too, according to Barb. Besides, you'll need some lunch in a few hours, and it's easy enough for me to come up."

"You already lost a lot of time yesterday."

"No, I didn't. I got through quite a bit of paperwork while you slept." Cameron stood up. "Which you probably need to do again, anyway. I'll check up on you in a while." He smiled. "Stop trying to get rid of me."

Deborah watched him go and had no idea if she felt regret or relief.

CAM WORKED nonstop for three hours, catching up on calls and the rest of his paperwork. The entire time, his conversation with Deborah kept buzzing in his head like a distant bee. Something about that conversation was important and particularly relevant to him.

What was it?

It was something besides the obvious fact that Deborah had never gotten over her father's desertion. That she was still angry with him. Hardly surprising, considering all the questions surrounding his departure.

Poor Deborah.

Not that she would want his sympathy. No, she'd clearly rather go around pretending to everyone that she was perfectly fine rather than accept any sympathy. Just like in the first few months he'd known her, when she'd been all smiley and chipper, never letting on that her fiancé had dumped her—

Cam drew a sharp breath. That was it. That was what bothered him.

Deborah had been deserted twice. First by her father and then by her fiancé. Two important men in her life, presumably the two most important, and both had walked out on her.

Rejection with a capital *R*.

Cam winced. It had to be a tough thing to get over. And he got the feeling Deborah hadn't dealt with it yet. That was bad news for her, but it was also bad news for him, because it meant that he would have to ignore his very strong attraction to her—okay, his rampant lust for her—and leave her alone.

He couldn't seduce the walking wounded. It wouldn't be moral or ethical.

Deborah needed a man who would stick with her for the long haul, and he wasn't that man. Hell, he didn't believe in *love,* never mind the everlasting, 'til-death-do-us-part *M* word.

He couldn't, *wouldn't,* be another man who left her.

Keeping his resolution would be the tough part. He'd be seeing a lot of Deborah, especially over the next few days. She had the flu and needed help, and he would be there for her. But he would not touch her, not now and not in the future. Even if she wore the slinkiest dresses to every event they attended together, he would not crack. Instead he'd grit his teeth and remember what he'd vowed right here in his office.

He would keep his hands off Deborah Clark.

Chapter Eleven

"That's not a word," Deborah said.

"Yes, it is." Cam picked out four new letter squares to replace the ones he'd just added to the Scrabble board. They were both sprawled out on the plush area rug in Deborah's living room, in front of the fire he'd lit in her fireplace.

Libby had curled up next to them on the couch. She was snoring again, and Cam grinned. If that cat intended to sleep off all the dinner scraps she'd eaten, she'd be napping until next year.

Deborah eyed him with obvious doubt. "I've heard of *thistle, whistle* and *mistle,* but *istle?*" Her smile was polite. "Aren't you missing a few tiles?"

Cam lifted a brow. "Are you suggesting I'm a few bricks short of a full load?"

She shrugged, but a hint of a smile played around her mouth. "What do you think?"

"I think you'd better decide if you're going to challenge me or not," Cam told her.

Deborah tilted her head, clearly considering it. Cam figured she wasn't going to bother, though. She looked too content. And even though she had a wicked cough, she looked a lot better than she had in the past several days. She was still a little pale, but some color had returned to her cheeks.

Plus, she was arguing with him, which had to mean her energy level was returning to normal. What a relief. Cam didn't even want to remember how listless and limp she'd been that first day. He must have several new gray hairs to mark that experience.

He'd probably have even more soon, for a different reason. These would be gray hairs caused by heroic and extremely painful self-restraint. A self-restraint that Deborah's stretchy, formfitting purple sweater was even now putting severely to the test. Again. In recent weeks she'd worn way too many sweaters and tops like this one for his comfort.

What the hell had happened to all those long, loose tunics?

His only comfort was that Deborah clearly had no idea of his struggle to control his baser instincts.

Cam grabbed the dictionary and flipped through it until he found the page. "I'll make it easy for you. Here we go—'*Istle,* a strong fiber from various tropical American plants.'" He showed her the entry.

"So it is." Deborah grinned up at him. "Very good." She took a leisurely sip of the lemon tea he'd made for her.

"Thank you."

"Even if it doesn't get you very many points," she teased.

"We aren't all after mere points," he informed her. "Some of us operate on a higher plane." *So high I'll probably get a nosebleed.*

She gave him a stare of exaggerated surprise. "Is that right?"

"Yes, that's right." Cam watched Deborah move

letter tiles around on her small wooden stand. She tried several different combinations, humming under her breath as she worked.

She looked happy. Beautiful, too. Her slight weight loss during her bout with the flu had added to the delicacy of her face, making her eyes look even bigger and her cheekbones a little more prominent. As usual, she wore very little makeup and, also as usual, it looked just right on her. Tonight her blond hair hung free, skimming her shoulders. It shone in the firelight, and Cam wanted to run his fingers through it.

Deborah arranged her pieces on the board with a triumphant air and Cam refocused his eyes. *"Quixotic,"* he read. "Hey, good job. That's… hmm…twenty-six points."

"And it's on a triple word score," she pointed out. "Seventy-eight."

Cam added it to her score and figured up totals. Then he winced. "You're killing me."

"No, I'm not. You're on a higher plane, remember?"

He laughed. He couldn't help it. She was smiling up at him, her chin tilted so that she looked like a mischievous little girl.

Except that her body was all woman, and so was the expression in those beautiful blue eyes.

Cam cleared his throat. "Speaking of high planes, how long have you been volunteering at Kids First?" For days he'd intended to ask her that question, but she had his brain so scrambled he could barely remember his own name.

"About five years, I guess, in one way or another. I've always wanted to help disadvantaged kids."

"Good for you. Have you always worked with the toddlers?"

She explained and he listened, impressed. She'd gotten involved with a lot of different projects. As she talked about the children, her face lit up. Enthusiasm filled her voice. It was clear she loved working with the kids.

"They're lucky to have you," Cam told her.

She lifted one shoulder and, for the first time that evening, looked uncomfortable. "I'm sure I get more out of it than they do. But with luck I'll manage to do something really memorable for them this spring."

"What's that?"

"I'm giving a party at the end of March. For all the kids. The kind of party where they can dress up in fancy clothes, play games, eat special treats and know that this party is just for them."

"That's great."

Deborah traced the fringe on her area rug with one index finger. "Most of us grew up taking parties for granted, you know? We went to all kinds of them, both our own and other kids', and we didn't see anything unusual in that. But most of these children barely get enough to eat. In fact, some of them *don't* get enough to eat. And although public aid has to be for necessities, every kid needs some fun memories."

Abruptly Deborah sat up. She shrugged. "That's what I'd like to help give them." She looked uncomfortable again, as if she thought she'd said too much. As if she figured he wouldn't be interested.

"I think that's the best idea I've heard in a long time," Cam said. "Can I help?"

"Help?" She looked confused. "You mean donate?"

He nodded. "Sure, I'll make a donation. But I want to help with the practical end of it, too, if you can use another volunteer. What are your plans for coming up with the food, the dress-up clothes and everything else for this party?"

Deborah's smile was pleased but cautious, as if she was happy about his offer but didn't want to count on it too much. "Ann's going to donate her services, as well as some of the food. Barb said she'll handle the photography. I may have one clothing supplier lined up, and I'm still working on getting a couple more."

"How many kids are there?"

"Somewhere around a hundred. We'll have to get a more exact number."

It was a small thing, but her use of the word *we* sent a small glow through Cam. Even though she might not have meant to include him in it, he chose to believe she did. And although Deborah might not expect much from him now, she'd soon learn she could count on him.

Guaranteed.

HER PHONE LIST was impossibly long. Deborah stared at it and hoped her voice was going to hold out. Phoning was the logical task to tackle since she still didn't feel up to tramping around in the latest snowfall to run errands. But she'd already spent a half hour on the phone with Ann, who was much sicker than Deborah had been and whose sister was taking care of her. With luck, Deborah had managed to cheer Ann up, but having such a croaky voice didn't help.

It was a good thing she had ample supplies of tea and cough drops. She had lots of everything, and she had to remember to reimburse Cameron. Assuming she had enough money to even come close. Her refrigerator and pantry had never been so well stocked.

She'd never eaten better, either. Who'd have thought Cameron would turn out to be such a good cook?

All in all, he'd taken excellent care of her for the past four days. Although she still couldn't remember much of Tuesday, she was fully aware of the time Cameron had spent with her for the rest of the week. He checked on her in the morning every day, showing up again to fix lunch and keep her company for a while. Then he reappeared in time to cook dinner. Afterward he built a fire in her fireplace and they either listened to music or played games. She'd never have figured Cameron for a fellow games lover, but the man was full of surprises.

Like his choice in gifts. She'd have guessed he was a roses kind of guy, the all-purpose perfect choice. Instead he'd brought her tulips, daffodils and other cheerful spring flowers. All obviously imported, since it was still too early for them. The riotous mass of color improved both her apartment and her spirits. And then there was her comfortable, plush new robe, another thoughtful gift.

Last night he had stunned her yet again by his interest in her Kids First party, an interest that apparently didn't stop at making a donation. It was easy enough to whip out a checkbook. After all, donating money was a snap for someone with plenty of it to spare. A willingness to donate time was a lot more rare, yet Cameron seemed prepared to do just that. His suggestion that he drum up some corporate sponsors and also help with the party games for the older kids was unbelievably exciting. In fact, she hadn't felt this overwhelmed since...since...

Since the last time Cameron had kissed her.

Deborah tapped a pencil impatiently. She shouldn't be thinking about that episode on her couch. In her weakened state, the excitement might be more than she could handle. Plus, she'd already vowed there would be no sexual involvement between herself and Cameron. All that was left was to inform him.

Or maybe she wouldn't have to. Recently Cameron hadn't touched her or shown any signs of a personal interest in her. Every once in a while she thought she saw something in his eyes, a look that made her heart start to pound, but then he'd glance away.

She was almost convinced she'd dreamed that interlude on her couch, that she'd totally imagined Cameron's passion and the urgency in his voice and his body. He'd seemed almost desperate to get her to acknowledge the desire they felt for each other.

Yet now, only a handful of days later, she had no idea how he felt about her. Maybe all the little details he'd discovered about her had been enough to change his mind. Maybe bright floral sheets and toothpaste squeezed from the middle were instant turnoffs for him.

Which would be entirely for the best. After all, the only thing more certain than death and taxes was the absolute lunacy of getting involved with Cameron Lyle.

CAM STARED OUT his office window. It was a large window, with a good view of the street and the nearby shops on that street. Usually Deborah was the only person capable of drawing his attention to his window, but he had come to a break in his paperwork just in time to see the elderly Mrs. Skirvin make her way into Sweetness and Light for what Cam now knew was her usual late afternoon chat.

Mrs. Skirvin was a client of his, but it was only over dinner last night that he'd found out about her habit of chatting with whoever she found at the café.

"Mrs. Skirvin likes to see familiar people. That's why she always picks Ann's café. Familiarity and force of habit. She's not the only one, either. Herbie probably only chases your other fish out of habit."

Cam blinked. Trying to follow Deborah's train of thought was a challenge.

"Sometimes even the ideas we have are the result of sheer force of habit." Deborah pointed her fork at him. "Take you and your views on love."

He flinched. "Do we have to?"

She'd given him a look accusing him of cowardice. "I bet you're only convinced that romantic love doesn't exist because you've thought that for so long."

"Not true. Even if it weren't for my parents' and the majority of my friends' divorces, all I'd have to do is look around. What do you call a fifty percent divorce rate?"

"I call it giving up too soon," she'd snapped.

Fortunately, she hadn't pursued the topic. Instead she'd gone on to list other practices she'd noticed among their neighbors. Cam could now remember only that Deborah's point about familiarity had something to do with how she felt the Kids First party should be presented to area merchants in order to gain their support. He'd lost touch with the details as he became more and more amazed at how much Deborah had learned about the people around them.

Habits and preferences were undoubtedly only one small aspect of what she knew about the merchants and residents of Tulip Tree Square. How many times had he watched from his office window as Deborah stood on the sidewalk and chatted with an elderly lady or a little boy and his dog? And that had been in the fall and early winter, when brisk weather didn't encourage long visits outside. No telling how chatty she got in the spring and summer.

When he'd first met her, Cam had interpreted her behavior as sheer nosiness and mindless chattering. But getting to know her had changed his perspective. Deborah genuinely liked people, which was undoubtedly why they responded so readily to her. What was boring small talk to him fascinated her, and people enjoyed her interest in them. Furthermore, as far as he knew, she'd never used her information about anyone in a malicious way.

Yes, no doubt about it. Deborah was impressive and alarming, all at the same time. Even though resisting her was one of the hardest things he'd ever done, it was probably a damned good thing he'd had to nix his idea about having an affair with her.

The problem was, he had to find the right way to back off. She'd been hurt enough. The last thing Deborah needed was another idiot blowing hot and cold on her. Last week he'd come on way too strong. After forcing her to admit her attraction to him, how the hell could he now tell her he'd changed his mind? *Sorry, sweetheart, I had no clue you were walking wounded. I can't risk hurting you again.* What kind of bigheaded jerk would say that?

But he had to think of something. Soon. Because he was running out of self-control. It was tough resisting Deborah's sexual allure, and then there was the woman herself. She was fun to be with. Even weak from the effects of the flu, Deborah Clark was more interesting, and more entertaining, than any woman he'd dated in recent memory.

Cam grimaced. He knew damned well that if he had any excuse at all for seeing her this weekend, he'd grab it and run. But he didn't, and that was both fortunate and unfortunate, depending on how he looked at it.

They had a cocktail party to go to together on Tuesday night. In fact, they had quite a few events on the calendar, and since he'd already told Deborah about every one, there was no getting out of them.

He could see it right now. There he'd be, standing by her side drinking wine and listening to a client's golf story, when the whole time he was dying to find the nearest bed, slide her dress off her and show her just how fantastic they would be together.

Worse, he'd now volunteered to help her with her Kids First party, which meant even more effort spent trying to resist her. Cam groaned. This was insane. Not only had he *not* gotten Deborah out of his system, his obsession with her had gone from bad to worse.

THE FOLLOWING Tuesday Deborah waited for Barb at a small table in Sweetness and Light. The scent of fresh banana nut muffins filled the air, and she had already succumbed to two of them. She had to build up her strength.

Lord, yes, give her strength.

Tonight she and Cameron had a cocktail party to

go to, and she was already a nervous wreck. Not because of the party itself, although that would have made sense. After all, many of Cameron's longest-standing clients would be there, and even if she didn't care about making more contacts, she wouldn't want to embarrass Cameron.

But right now she couldn't even think about the party. She couldn't get past the realization that she had not yet had that talk with Cameron, the one where she spelled out how disastrous it would be if they got involved. For all she knew, he thought they'd be picking up where they'd left off last Monday, when he'd dared her to deny her attraction to him and she'd been unable to do it.

Would Cameron expect to come home with her after the party?

Her palms dampened, but Deborah ignored them. It didn't matter what he expected. Besides, he hadn't been in touch with her all weekend, so he'd be unconvincing in the role of the desperate prospective lover.

Not that she'd missed him this weekend. It was only that after Cameron's cooking, the dinners stacked in her freezer had lost most of their appeal. And her morning crossword puzzles would have been more fun with his help. But all things considered, her weekend had been fine. Just fine. Peaceful, even.

"Hi, Deborah." Barb sat down opposite her at the tiny table, took off the woolen scarf that covered her gray curls and wrapped her hands around the mug of coffee Deborah had gotten her. "Thanks for the coffee. You look great. I still can't believe how fast you got over your bout with our nasty neighborhood flu bug. I was out nearly two weeks. What's your secret?''

Deborah gave her a wry smile. "Don't have one. Except maybe Cameron's cooking and both of your excellent care. Thanks again.''

The older woman shrugged. "I honestly didn't do much.''

"Of course you did. That whole first day had to have been intense.'' She still didn't remember much of it, and she probably wouldn't want to, either.

"Sure, but I was only there a total of an hour or so, mostly for moral support. Cam was in charge, and I must say, I've never seen the poor man look so worried. He was afraid you had something worse than the flu.''

"Really?'' Deborah wondered how someone in shock looked, and whether she looked that way right now.

Cameron had been with her all that day? Sponged her down? Taken care of heaven knew how many of her personal needs?

Oh, no.

Barb was nodding. "Oh, yes. Like I said, I've never seen him so worried. I guess that's why he called his own doctor in to examine you.'' She lifted her nose and sniffed. "Mmmm. Excuse me. I have to go get one of those cinnamon rolls just out of the oven. Do you want one?''

Absently, Deborah shook her head. She barely noticed Barb leave. She stared at the highly polished oak table top, concentrating on each knot and swirl.

Cameron had called in his own doctor? Had he really been that worried? Why hadn't he mentioned it to her?

As soon as the last thought hit her, so did the answer. Cameron knew she would insist on reimbursing him for the doctor visit. He also knew she didn't have much money.

Deborah traced a swirl in the wood. The question was, what did she do now? Confront him and ask him to give her the bill? If she did, Cameron would know Barb had mentioned it to her.

But the only alternative was to say nothing and let him pay her doctor bill.

Deborah was still thinking about it when Barb returned, carrying one of the enormous cinnamon rolls for which Sweetness and Light was so well-known. Deborah allowed herself to forget all about the topic for a while as she gave the other woman the latest news from Kids First and told her about Cameron volunteering to help find some more sponsors.

"I have a feeling he'd help you with just about anything, my dear." Barb's hazel eyes held a twinkle.

Deborah felt her cheeks heat. It was obvious what Barb thought, and Deborah couldn't enlighten her without sounding like the lady who protested too much. Besides, since Cameron had spent all that time nursing her back to health and had even brought in his own doctor, any denial Deborah voiced now wouldn't be believable.

"I must say, his taste has improved greatly." Barb smiled. "Now if I could just get him married off, I'd win my bet." She eyed Deborah.

"Don't look at me," Deborah said.

Barb only laughed.

DEBORAH STALKED into Cameron's office. "I am not going to have an affair with you."

He looked up from his desk. "Could you say that a little louder? I'm sure at least one person in Tulip Tree Square didn't hear you."

"Sorry," Deborah muttered. Now that she'd finally gotten it over with and her dread was gone, she felt like an idiot. And the blasted man wasn't helping. The least he could do was look disappointed or… or…*something*. But no, he just sat there watching her, all inscrutable. A Malibu Ken doll had more expression.

She sank into one of his client chairs. "The two of us want totally different things. You want sex with no strings attached, and I want a lifetime commitment. Not much common ground there."

"I guess not," Cameron said.

So that was it. Deborah hesitated a few seconds and then left his office, relieved to notice that Barb was still away from her desk. Slowly Deborah mounted the stairs to her apartment. She'd achieved exactly what she'd set out to accomplish.

Why was that so depressing?

WINEGLASS IN HAND, Cam leaned against the fireplace mantel in Henry Glassen's elegant sitting room and listened as his host described the best way to circumnavigate the pond on the area's newest golf course.

"Henry, only you could talk about golf at the end of February when we're under a foot of snow," said Michael Nates, another of Cam's clients.

"That's why I talk about it," retorted Henry. "It's a lot more entertaining than going to that lousy excuse for an indoor course."

Cam didn't hear much of the debate that followed.

Most of his attention was focused on Deborah, who stood a few yards away talking with a guy who looked straight off the cover of a men's fashion magazine. Cam had never seen him before, but he and Deborah seemed to have plenty to discuss, and what's-his-name clearly liked what he saw.

No wonder. Deborah's dark blue velvet dress was simple, but it followed the curves of her body in a way that made Cam's mouth go dry. The scoop neckline showed only a faint shadow of cleavage, just enough to bring up memories that he absolutely had to forget, no matter what else he did.

All evening Cam had fought his desire to touch her, and that velvet dress didn't help.

Neither did her hair. Deborah had left it down, but she'd curled the ends so it fell to her shoulders in soft golden waves that bounced a little when she turned her head. She would look spectacular wearing nothing but those curls. He wanted to see her like that. He wanted to wrap one of those curls around his finger. Hell, he wanted to take whole fistfuls of her silky hair and slide his fingers slowly through it while he—

Violently, Cam shut down his thoughts. He could not, *must not,* think about that. Not ever, but especially not right now, while he was surrounded by his oldest and most important clients. He couldn't afford to get lost in fantasies about Deborah.

Deborah. The woman who, only this afternoon, had rejected him in no uncertain terms.

He should be relieved. He should be jumping for joy that he no longer had to figure out a way to back off. Deborah had done it for him, which was a hell of a lot better solution. This afternoon, during the entire endless minute with her in his office, he'd made his face as neutral as he could get it and played Ping-Pong with two thoughts.

All for the best.

Damn, I want her.

Tonight's scenario was even worse than the one he'd conjured up in his imagination. Not only was he listening to golf chatter while he fought off his fantasies, he had Romeo over there, hanging on to Deborah's every word and practically drooling into his wine. Worse, she looked more than mildly interested in their conversation, too.

Or maybe she was just plain interested.

Cam shook his head. Not possible. Deborah had better taste than that. The guy wore suspenders, for God's sake. How could she be interested in someone that obnoxiously trendy?

How could she already be interested in another man when she'd kissed Cam back the way she had last week? When she'd unbuttoned his shirt, run her hands over his chest and arched her body up to meet his?

Cam stifled a groan. He had to get out of here. A few minutes outside in twenty-degree weather ought to do the trick.

Or he could take a header into the nearest snowdrift.

Chapter Twelve

"How long are you and Deborah going to keep up this foolishness?" Barb took her purse out of her desk and checked the money in her wallet.

Cam lifted a brow. "I have no idea what you're talking about."

His assistant looked up and laughed. "Sure you do. And you can drop the haughty stare, because I've known you too long for it to work on me."

"I'm going to get a new assistant," he muttered. "One who shows a little respect."

Barb ran a comb through her thick gray curls. "I have plenty of respect for you, as you well know. I'm fond of you, too, which in my book is worth even more. That's why I hate to see the two of you slinking around here avoiding each other like you've been doing for the past week."

Cam frowned. "I never *slink*."

"Okay, have it your own way. I'm going to lunch." Barb got up, collected her purse and headed for the door. "Just remember, if you've had a fight, someone has to apologize first." With those words, she grabbed her coat and disappeared.

Cam went back into his office. *A fight.* No, this

wasn't a fight. It was a cold war. Tit for tat. Deborah had rejected him as a lover, he'd ignored her at the party, and she'd flaunted Mr. Trendy. Deborah had said about two words to Cam all week.

Barb only thought it was a fight because she mistakenly believed they were involved. He had no claim on Deborah, which was why his desire to hang the yuppie puppy by his suspenders from a very high tree made no sense. Even if Cam had a legitimate claim on her, it would still make no sense. Jealousy was not an emotion he had experience, or patience, with. It wasn't his style.

But then neither was obsessing over a woman. Yet he dreamed about Deborah as he slept and daydreamed about her when he should be working.

Much as he hated to admit it, Barb was right. The silence between himself and Deborah was ridiculous, and the strain of it was undoubtedly why his mind was playing an ever-increasing number of unamusing tricks on him.

Time to put everything into perspective.

So what if Deborah found another man interesting? Just as well, since Cam couldn't give her what she needed. He'd have to check the guy out, naturally, but if he was okay, Cam would be happy for her.

Meanwhile, he'd do everything he could to restore the camaraderie they'd enjoyed while she was sick. Because the truth was, he'd missed Deborah over the past ten days. He liked having her around to eat meals and play board games with him. He even liked arguing with her. He'd never been enthusiastic about letting a woman share his personal space, and in fact until recently he never had.

But somehow it was different with Deborah, more

comfortable. Maybe because he felt he could be friends with her. He had occasional flashes of lust—okay, maybe more than occasional—but he managed to control them. All he had to do was keep controlling them. Knowing she was interested in someone else was bound to do the trick.

Cam glanced at his engagement calendar. He and Deborah had a business dinner to go to on Saturday night. That gave him only a few days to restore the atmosphere between them before they ended up with one hell of an uncomfortable evening out.

And before he himself went totally around the bend.

DEBORAH HUNG UP the phone and gave a little shriek. "Yes!" She danced a jig around the couch, causing Libby to open one eye and stare at her. The cat must have decided Deborah was a harmless lunatic, because she closed her eye again and went back to sleep.

Deborah wanted to sing and shout and dance. Two phone calls in the space of an hour, each bringing a new event planning job her way. Both prospective clients declared themselves delighted with her proposals. Both were faxing signed agreements immediately.

That meant she'd have to go down to Cameron's office to retrieve the faxes.

Deborah swallowed. When he'd suggested she use his fax machine, it hadn't occurred to her that she might ever be uncomfortable with that arrangement. But for much of last week, she'd avoided going downstairs, knowing she risked running into Cameron.

What a coward she was.

The whole thing was ridiculous. So she'd been hurt when he ignored her at the party. She had no right to resent Cameron's behavior. All week the situation had gotten more and more uncomfortable, and finally she'd avoided him completely.

But now she had to go get those faxes. It wasn't fair to make Barb bring them up.

A knock sounded. Deborah felt a mixture of relief and dismay. Obviously she was too late, because here was Barb. She flung open the door. "Sorry, Barb—"

"No Barb," said Cameron.

He stood outside her door in a watchful stance that suddenly reminded her of that time he'd shown up to challenge her about her use of his name as a fictional boyfriend. And once again, her apartment was way too small as soon as he stepped into it. He smelled like winter and pine trees. His cheeks were ruddy with the cold, so he must have just come back from lunch.

Cameron was carrying two sheets of paper and a small brown bag. He held out the papers. "Your faxes." His sudden smile surprised her, because it seemed tinged with uncertainty. "I'll confess I peeked. Congratulations."

"Thanks."

"I know Michael Nates, of course, but who's this guy Waller?"

"He's Jason's father." When Cameron still looked blank, she added, "I met Jason at the party last Tuesday." She didn't really want to think about that party, but at least it had gotten her two clients.

He frowned. "Jason's the guy with the suspenders?"

She smiled. "Was that a grimace? I know, that was my reaction, too. He's fun to talk with, though."

"Are you going to go out with him?" Cameron's eyes were unreadable.

Deborah was shocked at how tempted she was to lie and say yes. And she was dismayed at how badly she wanted to know that it mattered to Cameron if she dated someone else.

But she wasn't willing to lie to him. "No."

Cameron smiled.

After more than a week of strained politeness, the sight of his smile made her throat tighten. She'd missed it.

She missed Cameron.

"Looks like business is booming," he commented.

"It's a lot better than it was, thanks to the contacts I've made through you." It was the truth. She owed all her new business to Cameron, at least indirectly. If it weren't for the parties and other events they'd attended, she would never have met any of the people who'd become clients.

"I'm glad it's working. Shall we toast your success?" He handed her the brown bag he'd been holding. Inside she found a box of imported gingersnaps, the same brand her sister had sent. When she looked up again he was grinning. "I figure I've eaten all of yours."

She laughed. It felt better than she could ever have imagined to be back on a friendly footing with Cameron. "I'll make some coffee," she said.

"Herbal tea is fine. I'm cutting back on caffeine."

Deborah shot him a quick glance and received an innocent smile in return.

"How's that going?" She busied herself getting

tea bags. No point looking for meaning where there wasn't any. He probably didn't even remember her suggestion two months ago.

"You mean, am I getting less grumpy?" Amusement filled his voice. He leaned on the doorjamb leading into the kitchen. "I really couldn't say."

"No, that's not what I mean. Are you feeling less stress? That's the important thing." Deborah stifled a grimace. As he himself had pointed out, these days she wasn't exactly a model of stress-free living. Getting mixed up with Cameron Lyle had turned her calm, cheerful world upside down. Even now, she was a lot more aware than she wanted to be of his presence in her small kitchen.

"Am I feeling less stress?" Cameron repeated her question in thoughtful tones. "Hmm. No, I'd have to give you a definite negative on that one." Something in his voice, in addition to the intensity with which she could feel his gaze on her, made Deborah's cheeks warm. She was careful to keep her back to him as she finished tea preparations.

"Where did you find these ginger cookies? Locally or on one of your trips? I've never seen them anywhere around, even though I always look, because I think they go better than any other cookie with tea." She was babbling. Had he picked up on her nerves? Deborah turned around.

He had. But he didn't comment. "I found them right here in Indy." He told her where as they took their tea and cookies into her living room. "So now you won't have to rely on your sister to supply you." He paused. "What did you say her name is?"

"Julie." Deborah smiled.

"Judging by your photos, she looks a lot like you."

"That's what everyone says. She's a couple of years younger than me." Still, people usually guessed wrong on their birth orders.

"You're close, aren't you? The two of you, I mean?"

"Very, although our personalities are pretty different. Julie's more like my mom."

"And you're like your father?" Cameron was watching her.

"Yes."

We're two of a kind, kiddo.

You're so stubborn, Deborah.

She took a quick little breath. "When we were kids, Julie used to tag along after me constantly. Most of the time I didn't mind." She chuckled. "This is a really unsisterly thing to say, but she was a cute, good-natured little girl." A little girl who, at eleven, had still been happy and sweet during the last few months of their father's life. Unlike Deborah, who had metamorphosed into a temperamental, difficult teenager, Julie had given their father nothing but joy.

And how tough it was not to envy her that.

"Tell me more about Sally," Deborah said.

Cameron's eyes registered her change of subject, but he only smiled. "You'll have to meet her some time."

They were halfway through their tea when Cameron brought up the subject of the Saturday night business dinner. "Pat Belen lives a few blocks from me. If I came to get you at about six, we could stop by my place on the way, and I could show you the progress I've made on games for the teenagers."

"You're already working on games?"

"Sure. That's the fun part." He grinned. "The

sponsor stuff is a lot duller, although I've made some progress there, too. I'll tell you all about it Saturday.''

It was an offer she couldn't resist. She was intensely curious about what Cameron had come up with for games. The fact that she'd be going to his house to see them wasn't a big deal. After all, she'd been there before, and it wasn't as if they'd be staying long, anyway.

''That's fine,'' she agreed. ''But I should just drive over to your house. It doesn't make sense for you to come all the way into town for me when the dinner is out by your place.'' Of course, Cameron would never have suggested that solution himself. He was far too polite for that.

The realization made her briefly wonder again about his uncharacteristic behavior at last week's cocktail party. But then Deborah shook off the thought. They were both going to forget all about the last few days.

''I don't mind coming to get you,'' Cameron told her.

''Well, I mind it. I'll come there, which is a lot more efficient.'' Plus, she would feel better being in control of her own transportation. It wasn't Cameron she didn't trust, it was herself. She didn't want to be tempted to ask him up to her apartment when he dropped her off. She didn't want the evening to feel in any way like a date.

''Okay, if that's how you want to do it, then I'll see you at my place around six.''

WHEN HIS DOORBELL RANG, Cam hurried to answer it. Not because he couldn't wait to see Deborah, of course, but because it was damned cold for the middle of March. No point in making her stand out there on his porch longer than she had to.

"Hi." *How stunningly original.*

"Hi, yourself." She hurried in, shivering. No wonder, since her black shawl was incredibly flimsy. It looked fantastic, especially with her blond hair cascading over it, but the thing couldn't be worth much in this kind of cold weather. What was the woman trying to do, have a relapse?

When she took off the shawl, Cam forgot all about relapses. He forgot every other damned thing, too.

Deborah wore basic black. Her dress was chic, classic and formfitting. With it, she wore sheer black stockings.

Very sheer black stockings.

This was the first time Cam had seen those mile-long legs encased in black hose, and the sight made his mouth dry up. From the hem of her dress to her sexy black heels, those legs were perfection. Add to them her full, rosy lips, and he was in deep trouble.

The really weird thing was, black hose had never done much for him before. Neither had red lipstick. He appreciated them, of course, but he'd never gone into meltdown over them, and it wasn't like he hadn't seen both on plenty of beautiful women. Maybe it was the way Deborah wore the stockings and the lipstick, as if she was completely unaware of how gorgeous she looked.

"Bring on the games," Deborah said with a grin when he'd hung up her shawl.

"How about a drink first?" He damned well needed one.

By the time he'd shown her his various game ideas, which included sporting competitions, modified board games and just about everything else he remembered from his own childhood party experiences, Cam felt more comfortable. He lay sprawled out on the floor of his office, and Deborah sat in an armchair. She didn't look comfortable, but at least she was less wary than before, when he'd led her upstairs.

He wasn't sure what her reluctance meant. All he knew was that usually, women were a lot more interested in seeing his house than he was in showing it to them. Since Deborah was one of very few women he'd invited to his house, her reaction was more disappointing than he wanted to admit.

Still, sharing the games he'd come up with was fun, and he found her enthusiasm gratifying.

"These are terrific. The kids are going to have a wonderful time." Her eyes shone with approval and excitement. "Thanks for doing such a great job."

"I had fun with it." Cam couldn't seem to look away. His gaze met hers and he was lost in her eyes, lost in the emotions he read there. He saw happiness and admiration. He also saw a sexual awareness that started his heart pounding. And there was something else, too, something he couldn't identify but that made his throat tighten.

He forgot where they were. He forgot what they were doing. All he wanted was to kiss her, and he wanted that so badly he could feel his hands trembling. His gaze dropped to her mouth.

And then Deborah jumped up from her armchair. "I guess we should be heading to the dinner party soon."

Cam stared at her, trying to process what she'd said. Then he got up, too. It was a damned good thing Deborah had moved when she had. He'd come within inches of pulling her down onto the carpet with him, and that would have been a mistake.

Cam drew a deep breath. Every muscle of his body ached.

Taking their drinks with them, they made their way down the hall. As they passed his bedroom, he saw Deborah take another quick, curious glance. A guilty expression immediately crossed her face, but Cam felt a strong sense of satisfaction at her interest. He gave only partial attention to her questions about the hosts of the dinner party. Deborah chattered all the way downstairs.

I only gab when I'm nervous. Cam could hear her wry voice admitting it to him. Did she remember?

One thing was for sure. She felt the same sexual tension he did. He could see it in her face and read it in her body movements. It was there in her overly bright voice, too.

All they could do was ignore it.

"I'll be right back," Cam told her when they got downstairs. "Why don't you make yourself comfortable in the living room for a minute?" Or five or six. That was probably about how long it would take to talk some sense into himself. While he was at it, he could start the dishwasher.

And pour the rest of his drink down the sink. He needed a clear head.

When Cam emerged from the kitchen, Deborah was standing in the corner of the living room staring at his fish in apparent fascination. "Hey, look at that. Herbie's stopped terrorizing everybody in the tank."

"Really?" He crossed over to join her.

"I think the hunter has become the hunted." Her voice held both surprise and amusement.

Herbie hovered around the large rock at one end of the tank, looking as if he was hiding. Then a bright blue angelfish rounded the corner, saw him, and made a sudden dash straight at him. Herbie fled. As Cam and Deborah watched, the two fish repeated this sequence several more times.

Cam stared at the angelfish. "I guess Herbie's the only one he's chasing."

"Yep. Revenge," said Deborah.

"Looks like it."

"Doesn't that seem like a people kind of thing to do? I could be wrong, but I don't think revenge is usually a motivator in the animal kingdom." Deborah stared into the tank. "You know, Cameron, your fish are more interesting than I ever considered fish could be."

He grinned. "I wouldn't get too carried away with the comparisons."

"What do you mean?"

"I don't think there are many parallels to be drawn between fish and people."

She chuckled. "No, possibly not. Especially not with fish like yours."

Cam frowned at her. "What do you mean, fish like mine? There's nothing wrong with my fish. A couple of them are a little eccentric, that's all."

"Maybe. But if you ask me, your fish are more confused than anything else. They don't seem to have any sense of solidarity. They've never been in the wild, so they don't have an accurate picture of the friend-foe distinction." Deborah smiled cheerfully. "Now, if Libby were here, she'd sort them out."

He eyed her. "Sort them out?"

"She likes fish."

Cam winced. "I can't believe you're standing here in my living room, drink in hand, threatening my fish."

"I'm not threatening them. I was only thinking out loud."

He sent her a level stare. "Maybe silent thinking will work better for both of us."

"I meant Libby enjoys looking at fish." Deborah cleared her throat. "I really wasn't suggesting she would eat them."

Cam looked at her. Her blue eyes were open wide. When he gazed into them, he came close to forgetting what they were talking about.

"Okay," he said finally. "I can accept that. After all, it's not as if they're in any danger from Libby, anyway. To get at them, she'd have to reach into all that water cats find so yucky." He smiled.

"Oh, the water wouldn't be a problem." Her voice held confidence.

Cam frowned. "It wouldn't?"

"No. Libby's actually pretty fond of water. When I brush my teeth, she always wants to bat the stream around. One time, she hopped into the shower with me, but I think the spray was too forceful for her." Deborah's smile held fond memory. "She doesn't like to get her whole body wet, just her paws and sometimes her head. Between you and me, I think it's the motion of the water that fascinates her more than the water itself."

Cam watched her for a long moment. "Your cat dabbles in water and you're calling my fish weird?"

"She doesn't dabble. Libby always has a goal."

"Like snagging a few fish," Cam suggested dryly. Deborah's eyes met his. She looked as if she'd love to deny it. But they both knew Libby would find his fish fascinating.

"I don't think she would eat them," Deborah said finally. "But she might play with them for a while..."

"*Stop.*" He shuddered. "Let's talk about something else."

"Okay. What do you suggest?"

Cam hesitated. They could talk about something light. Or he could ask Deborah the question he'd wanted to ask ever since she'd told him about her father. Should he risk asking it? He hated to upset her. On the other hand, much to his surprise, he really needed to know.

"I have one question for you," he told her.

"Shoot."

It wasn't as easy as that. Cam searched for words. "I just wondered how you can believe so strongly in marriage. I mean, look at all the conflict it creates."

"No, it doesn't—"

"Okay, we disagree on that, and I admire your confidence. I don't understand it, though, especially since your own parents..." He trailed off, unable to find the right words.

"You mean, because my dad left," she finished for him.

"Right."

"I see your point. But marriage doesn't create the conflict you're talking about. That's already there." She gave a wry smile. "Marriage just raises the stakes. And that's a positive thing, because if the stakes are too low, where's the motivation to keep trying?"

Cam shook his head.

Deborah traced the rim of her wineglass. "I don't

think my father left because of my mother. I've never doubted that they loved each other, and neither has she. But he had a stressful job, and I hear that teenage daughters are also stressful.'' She smiled, but the smile didn't reach her eyes.

He frowned.

Deborah put her glass down. ''Thanks for the wine, but shouldn't we be going? We'll be late to this dinner unless we hurry.''

Cam watched her. She looked too cheerful. She also sounded too cheerful. But the conversation was over, that much was clear. At least for now. Besides, as Deborah had pointed out, they had to go.

The scary thing was, he'd forgotten all about the dinner.

A WEEK LATER Deborah surveyed the large reception hall with satisfaction. The bride and groom had already been safely dispatched on their honeymoon, but their guests showed no signs of slowing down on the dance floor. The whole event had gone off flawlessly, from the wedding ceremony to the elaborate reception.

It was a fitting way to end her career as a wedding planner. Thanks to the new clients she'd acquired, she could finally devote herself to other types of events.

''Let me guess.'' Ann appeared suddenly, looking so energetic it was hard to believe she'd only recently recovered from the flu. ''You're grinning because you've just won a date with the Hollywood heartthrob of your choice.''

''Nope.''

''Oh, silly me.'' Ann slapped her hand to her forehead. ''You don't need Hollywood because you've

already got our own local heartthrob in your pocket.''
She gave a teasing grin.

Deborah shook her head. "No, I don't.''

And that was the truth. No woman would ever have
Cameron Lyle in her pocket. When he said he didn't
believe in love or marriage, the man was not kidding.
He obviously felt very strongly about the whole issue.
His reasoning was flawed, of course, but with his history that wasn't a complete surprise. Everyone had
emotional blind spots.

Unfortunately, Cameron's were extremely depressing. Not *personally* depressing, of course. No, she just
felt bad for him, because he was going to miss out
on so much in life that was really good.

Ann was giving her the skeptical look she'd mas-
tered so well. "Oh, come on. The man kisses you like
there's no tomorrow, painstakingly nurses you back
to health, drowns you in flowers and even buys you
lingerie, and you don't have him hooked?''

Deborah stared at her. "How did you find out about
all that?'' This was the first time she'd seen Ann since
her friend had gotten up and about again. And even
if Deborah had seen her, she wouldn't have given
Ann those details.

They didn't mean anything. Or at least, not what
her friend thought.

Ann smiled. "Tell me about the lingerie. I want to
live vicariously.''

Deborah raised her eyes to the ceiling. "You mean
Stella didn't give you details? Someone's got to tell
the woman she's slipping.''

"Come on, *give*. Lace, ribbons?''

"No, plain cotton.'' Deborah laughed at her

friend's expression. "He got me a comfortable, very modest lounging robe. See? Nothing gossip worthy."

"I don't agree. That only proves he doesn't think of you as some generic chickie-poo."

Deborah stifled a grimace. *Chickie-poo?* No, that was definitely not how he saw her. What was the saying? Oh, yeah. *Be careful what you ask for because you might get it.*

She sighed. She'd wanted Cameron Lyle to see her as a person, and he did. He liked her, she could tell. He enjoyed her company. He even understood her, about as much as she figured any male could.

But Cameron didn't think of her as a woman. Not anymore. And why should he? He'd seen her at her absolute worst. She could have saved herself the embarrassment of telling him she wouldn't have an affair with him.

He didn't want her, anyway.

Except, of course, when she was right in front of his nose at the wrong time. Like last Saturday, when he'd almost kissed her. At first she'd been so stunned she couldn't move, but then she'd realized she couldn't let Cameron kiss her simply because she was looking presentable for once and he was in a romantic mood. After all, this was a man who, as far as she knew, hadn't had a girlfriend in months. For a virile, healthy guy like Cameron, that kind of sexual frustration had to be hard to take.

"You know something?" Ann was watching her. "I think you've got a confidence problem. I think you had it even before Mark the Unworthy did a bunk."

"I do not." She had plenty of confidence. In fact, she had every confidence in the world that Cameron was way out of her league.

Ann narrowed her eyes. "Are you still claiming you're not interested in him?"

"I'm not claiming anything. Have you got all the info you need to cater the Kids First party?" Deborah kept her voice even.

Ann's eyes narrowed, and for a moment she was silent. "I think so," she said finally. "We've got the menu items and quantities taken care of, so we're good to go. How are you doing with everything else?"

"Great. Games for all ages are finished, music and prizes are almost ready, and Cameron found the last party clothes supplier for us yesterday." Deborah frowned. She most definitely should not have brought up his name.

Sure enough, Ann jumped on it. "He's been a very *devoted* volunteer, wouldn't you say?"

Deborah gave a purposely vague smile. "I'd say he's been a big help. So have you. I'd also say it's a good thing we're keeping this party simple, or else we'd never be ready a mere two weeks from now."

"I guess we'll have to put off the rest of this conversation." Ann fixed her with a meaningful look. "Right now I'd better get back to the kitchen."

Deborah watched her go with a guilty relief. She knew Ann wanted more details of what she was convinced was a romance in the making. But Deborah didn't have any to give her, because there was no romance between herself and Cameron Lyle.

And there never would be.

Chapter Thirteen

Her fast food dinner was a mistake.

Deborah stared at the lone burger sitting on her coffee table. Spread out next to her on the couch, in a messy jumble, was the day's newspaper, complete with a lot more coupons exactly like the one she'd just used.

Buy One, Get One Free.

Two for $3.

She'd already tossed her extra burger into the freezer, and she had absolutely no desire to eat the remaining one.

One. A lonely number.

This was Cameron's fault. In the past few weeks, he'd shown her how much fun a man could be. He'd cooked for her, laughed with her and played endless board games with her. They'd eaten dinner together nearly every night, after which they'd worked on the Kids First party, now just eight days away.

Eight days, then the camaraderie would be gone.

In a few weeks, Cameron himself would be gone. After their last event together, he'd be out of her life.

It was a depressing thought. In spite of the sexual tension right beneath the surface, Cameron was easy to be with. And because of that tension, having him around made life more exciting than ever before. How strange that she hadn't had either the ease or the excitement with Mark, a man she'd known for years and had even planned to marry. A man whose mother she was so fond of.

She ought to check in with Marilyn. She'd neglected her, and she missed the older woman's gentle humor.

It took Deborah only the space of their "hellos" to realize her motherly friend was not her usual cheerful self.

"Mark's *eloped*." Marilyn gave a muffled sob. "He just called me. I barely know the girl! We've met once. Mark only met her two months ago. I don't understand their rush. He swears she's not pregnant, that they just knew right away they wanted to get married. But he's not thinking, and I'm so afraid he's going to be sorry later."

Deborah managed a few sympathetic murmurs, but her mind wasn't on them. Mark was married? Already? It had barely been four months since he broke up with Deborah. If he weren't so honest, she'd assume he'd met this other girl long before. But Mark never lied.

Marilyn took an audible breath. "Oh, Deborah, how thoughtless of me to blurt it out like that. I'm sorry, I'm just...upset."

"Naturally. And don't worry. I'm fine, Marilyn."

"Of course you are. Your young man is wonderful." Her voice held a wistful note.

Deborah grimaced. Obviously, this wasn't the time to set Marilyn straight. "Do you want me to come over?"

"Thank you, dear, but Mark's father should be here within the hour. Ex-husband or not, he's still a support system, and Howard is even less happy about this than I am."

Deborah did her best to cheer Marilyn up, but when she got off the phone she could feel all her determined cheerfulness slide away. She sat very still on her sofa, trying to take it all in.

Mark, married.

Mark, who had dated her for two years before proposing, and who had broken up with her in the middle of what would have been a fifteen-month engagement, was now married to a woman he'd met only two months ago.

Deborah stared at a sofa cushion without really seeing it and tried to ignore the ache in her throat. All this time she'd told herself Mark had backed out of marrying her simply because he was unable to commit to marriage right now. She'd told herself it had nothing to do with her, personally, that it could have happened to anyone.

But she'd been wrong.

It wasn't that Mark didn't want to get married. It was simply that he didn't want to marry *her*.

Deborah's eyes stung. Hurt piled onto loneliness.

The touch of a cold nose, followed by a weight in her lap, announced Libby's presence. Her cat gave her a grave look and a small lick on her wrist. Deborah sank her fingers into the animal's soft fur.

Why was she so depressed? Not because of Mark himself. If he had ten wives, it wouldn't matter to her. Still, rejection was rejection, and Mark's suddenly felt way more personal. He hadn't rejected *marriage*, he'd rejected *her*.

What was wrong with her? Why had every man who'd ever been important to her—her dad, Rick, Mark—left? Whatever her flaw was—and what if there was more than one?—maybe it explained why Cameron—

No. Deborah drew in a breath. She was *not* going there. It didn't matter why Cameron no longer desired her. It didn't matter, because for him a sexual relationship with her would have meant only that—sex.

Deborah took a long breath and stared out the window. It was raining. In fact, it was pouring, the sky filled with long silver sheets of spring rain that she'd have enjoyed watching on any other evening.

Tonight, however, she was more depressed than she'd ever been in her life. What was she going to do about it? No point in moping around her apartment feeling sorry for herself, and in any case, she was out of chocolate.

Chocolate. Yes, that was it. She would go shopping and buy chocolate. And a dress. Or maybe not a dress, since her budget was shot to Hades, but she would buy something fun, like parrot earrings or a hula hoop. And she would wear cheerful, comfortable clothes, water-friendly clothes, for her shopping trip in the rain.

Who said you couldn't have fun when you were depressed?

CAM TOOK OFF his reading glasses and pinched the bridge of his nose. He flipped his financial magazine closed. That venerable publication might be the last word in financial forecasting, but right now all the words were running together, which meant it was time to quit. Time to eat, too, judging by the rumbling of his stomach.

Had Deborah eaten yet?

He was shutting off the computer in the break room when he heard the high whine of the fax machine. Several seconds later, Cam smiled and looked at his watch. Six-thirty. With luck, he would catch Deborah in.

Her lights were on. His heart beating faster than he wanted to acknowledge, Cam knocked on her door.

"Deborah? I've got a fax for you."

The door opened a few seconds later, and there she stood. What he could see of her, anyway. She wore a bright yellow slicker with a huge hood, and since the hood was up, her face was almost completely hidden. The bottom half of her featured fuchsia leggings and an ancient pair of running shoes she must have dug out of the back of her closet.

"Thanks." Deborah took the fax from him and stashed it without even looking at it. "I'd, um, invite you in, but as you can see, I'm just about to head out..."

Her voice sounded strange. Muffled and lifeless, somehow. Cam peered at her, but he could barely see her. Alarm flashed through him. "What's wrong?"

"Wrong? What makes you think anything's wrong?"

"You don't sound like yourself." He stared hard into her eyes, as if he could read in them what he needed to know. But her eyes seemed lifeless, too, and that worried him even more than her voice. Why was she upset? And why was she trying to hide it from him? Most troubling of all, why did her attempts bother him so much?

"I just need a drink of water and a cough drop." She slapped back her hood and disappeared into the bathroom.

She had a cold? Cam shook his head. Deborah didn't look sick. She looked depressed.

Cam invited himself in and looked around for clues. Newspapers all over the sofa and a lone burger sitting on the coffee table didn't tell him much, except that she'd apparently been about to leave without eating her dinner, if you could call a burger dinner.

What the hell happened?

"Okay, that should do it," she announced. Giving him a maniacally cheerful grin, Deborah breezed by him, heading for the door.

He put out an arm to stop her. "Where are you going?"

"Shopping."

"Without your dinner?" He pointed to the burger.

"Oh, that. Well, I'm not hungry. I'll put it in the freezer with the other one, and they can be company for each other. I really need to get going. I have a lot of chocolate to buy."

Cam stared at her. "Chocolate?" She was going out into torrential rain to buy chocolate?

"Yes, and parrots." She frowned. "What did I do with my purse?"

"I don't know." He wasn't going to help her find it, either. This woman shouldn't be going anywhere right now.

"Oh, yes, the bathroom." Deborah marched back into it.

Cam watched her go and thought fast. She clearly didn't want to talk about it, but underneath her aggressively cheerful façade was one very upset woman. Her eyes held a lost look that made his chest hurt.

He couldn't let her go out all alone.

Deborah came back into the living room carrying her purse. The alarmingly cheerful grin was back on her face.

"Hey, come have dinner at my place with me," Cam said in a gentle, deliberately casual voice. "I've got Swedish meatballs in the Crock-Pot, so all we have to do is cook the noodles and make a salad. How does that sound?"

She looked at him, her smile fading and hesitation creeping into her eyes.

"I've got chocolate, too." He had to have some stashed somewhere, and he would find it if he had to tear apart his kitchen. Of course, he couldn't promise her parrots, but they could find a pet shop.

"You have chocolate?" Deborah bit her lower lip.

Cam nodded. "Come on, let's go. After dinner we can play some games." He'd make sure she won, too. He'd cheer her up if it was the last thing he did.

"Okay," Deborah said.

Cam shepherded her out of her apartment and downstairs.

"I'll meet you there," she suggested.

Let her drive? No way. "I'd rather have your company. I'll bring you back." To his relief, she didn't argue.

Together they dashed out. Deborah allowed him to install her in the front seat of his car, the same car she'd once offered to wash for a month as a substitute for serving as his hostess. The memory of his horror would have amused him if he weren't so damned worried about Deborah.

What was wrong? Was it bad news, and if so, was it about her, or somebody else? Was she sick, maybe really sick? Cam felt stirrings of fear but clamped down on them. He had to help Deborah. He had to wipe the lost look from her eyes. He wanted her to laugh and be happy. He wanted to see joy light up her beautiful blue eyes. He would do anything in his power to accomplish that.

"How about a little wine?" Cameron held up a bottle of burgundy and two wineglasses. His expression matched the relaxed atmosphere of his kitchen. The room was cozier than she remembered, with hanging copper pots and several ivy plants.

"Sounds good." At her first sip, warmth filled her. Cameron was watching her with a sharp gaze that probably saw too much, but Deborah couldn't work up any concern over it. She would rather be here with him than shopping, no matter how much chocolate she might have bought. In fact, she would rather be here with Cameron than any other place she could imagine, except she was a lot better off not thinking about that.

And not thinking about how good he looked in the black jeans and cream corduroy shirt he'd changed into. His hair was still damp from the rain, its ends curling in a way that made her want to touch it.

Her gaze met his. Suddenly afraid of what he might be able to read in her eyes, Deborah turned her attention back to the salad she was supposed to be making.

"Okay, what else should I chop up here?"

"We've got tomato, cucumber, red onion and carrot still to go in." He lined them all up on the counter for her. "That ought to do it."

"Great. I like the piano music." It was true, even though she said it mostly as a distraction. "Very relaxing."

He smiled. "Well, it's a lot more mellow than The Rolling Stones, that's for sure."

"Hey, that's vintage, quality stuff," Deborah protested. "Symbolic of a great era."

"An era you never lived in."

He wasn't going on about her age again, was he? "Neither did you."

"That's right. And from what I've seen and heard, we didn't miss much." He laid a loaf of French bread on the counter.

"That's a typical Mr. Conservative thing to say. And so what if I wasn't there for the sixties? You think only people who lived through an experience feel nostalgia?"

Cameron shook his head. "Not at all. I'd guess most nostalgia is the result of *not* having had an experience."

She eyed him. "Exactly. So what's your point?"

"I don't know." He grinned. "I'm not sure I had one. But it's fun arguing with you, anyway."

"Oh, well, in that case, we could always talk some more about the weird psyche of your fish."

Cameron winced. Then he pointed his bread knife at her. "You leave my fish alone."

"Coward," she teased, admiring his easy motions as he buttered half of the loaf and stuck it in the oven. They'd been here less than half an hour, yet although she felt a small ache in her chest every once in a while, she wasn't in deep distress anymore.

She felt comfortable fixing dinner with Cameron in his kitchen. In the darkness outside the kitchen window, the rain fell, now gently. Deborah listened to the soft, steady rhythm. This was the first time they'd fixed dinner in his kitchen, yet it felt like they cooked together all the time. If she believed in reincarnation or past lives, she'd probably be convinced they *had* done this many times.

Deborah looked up from the tomato she was slicing just in time to catch Cameron's gaze on her. What must he be thinking? He'd come up to her apartment and she'd babbled away about chocolate and parrots and who knew what else. She herself had no idea, since she hadn't paid any attention to what she was saying. No wonder Cameron had whisked her away. He'd probably been terrified of what she might do behind the wheel.

Even though she wasn't babbling anymore, she must still look pretty crazy. On the other hand, fuchsia leggings and a cutoff tie-dye sweatshirt would do that for anyone.

At least she had her emotions firmly under control now.

CAM MADE HIMSELF WAIT all through dinner, which Deborah ate with the same gratifying enthusiasm she'd shown when he cooked for her at her apartment. She had second helpings of everything. She drank more wine, too, although he was careful not to fill her wineglass all the way to the top.

He didn't want her so foggy she wasn't able to tell him what the hell was going on. He had to know the answer to that question. He *needed* to know. It had nothing to do with curiosity and everything to do with the simple fact that he never wanted to see Deborah look like that again, all hurt and bruised in spirit.

Cam waited some more, keeping up his end of a light conversation touching on sports, books and movies.

"That was incredible." Deborah sat back with a sigh. "Too bad I can't get you to cook me dinner every night." As soon as she'd said it, her cheeks went almost as pink as her leggings.

"You don't cook at all?"

"Only in dire emergency."

Cam listened to her horror stories with amusement, but part of his mind kept replaying her wistful comment. Funny, but Deborah was the only woman he'd ever met who he could actually imagine cooking dinner for every day.

Usually he didn't even invite the women he dated to his house, never mind cook for them. He'd always figured letting a woman into his personal space would give her too many ideas, besides being an invasion of his privacy. But having Deborah here didn't feel like an invasion. It somehow seemed only normal. Natural.

"I guess we all have our talents, but cooking isn't mine." She gave him a rueful smile.

"Eating is, though," he teased. "Don't you want to know what's for dessert?"

Her eyes lit up, but then she groaned. "I'm not sure. I'm stuffed." She waited two seconds. "Okay, what is it?"

"Beats me. Something chocolate."

"Really?"

"Sure. You wanted chocolate, remember?" He'd almost forgotten, himself, because she looked so much better. Nothing like the woman he'd brought home with him. In fact, she looked enough like the usual Deborah that his protective instincts were in danger of submerging as his hormones woke up again.

She busied herself clearing off the table. "Oh, right." She wasn't looking at him. She made two trips into the kitchen and back before her gaze met his. "So what forms of chocolate do you have?"

"Chocolate chips and cocoa powder, at least that I know of. I'll dig and see if I have anything else." Assuming he could get his mind off the sexy curve of her slender thighs and calves. Those leggings fit her way too well. And her bright tie-dye floral sweatshirt was too short to cover them. It barely covered her midriff. From time to time he caught tantalizing glimpses of skin he knew from experience was smooth and soft. And he was pretty sure she wasn't wearing a bra.

Cam frowned. Wrong time for these thoughts.

He dug, but found no other promising avenues. "We could make chocolate chip cookies. Or, if you want something more intense, we could do shakes or a mousse."

"Chocolate mousse? You know how to make that?"

"Sure. Don't look impressed. It's really easy. All we need are the chocolate chips, a little water and some eggs. And time for the mousse to set, although we can hurry it along by putting it in the freezer." He grinned. "Ten minutes' prep time."

She smiled back. "My kind of dessert."

AN HOUR and a half later they had finished making the mousse, played several rounds of checkers and eaten their dessert, which Deborah swooned over. But she had not brought up the topic he most wanted to discuss. And Cameron finally realized she didn't intend to.

Which left him with no choice. He couldn't wait any longer, and he also didn't want her imagining that whatever was bothering her didn't matter to him.

"What happened today?" Cam asked quietly as they sat on his living room sofa finishing their decaf. Beethoven played softly in the background.

Deborah looked at him, her eyes wary. "Happened?"

He knew then that it wasn't going to be easy, not that he'd ever thought otherwise.

Cam kept quiet. He wasn't going to twist her arm, however badly he needed to know. He cared too much about his own privacy to run rampant over someone else's, especially Deborah's. So he drank his coffee and tried not to imagine too many dire scenarios.

"Mark's married." The words fell like stones into the silence.

Cam didn't know what he'd expected, but it wasn't this. Not flat tones and calm eyes darkened with what might have been grief.

Not his own breath, sharp and suddenly hurting his lungs.

And definitely not the voice inside him, echoing over and over with a violence that shocked him.

You can't be in love with him.

"I called Marilyn for a chat, and she told me he'd just eloped. He meets this woman and two months later, pouf!" Deborah snapped her fingers. "He marries her. You know how long he and I dated before we got engaged? Two years. *Two.* And then he couldn't go through with it. Of course, it was a good thing, but—''

"It was?" His voice was a croak. Cam cleared his throat.

She frowned. "Yes, of course. I already told you that. I'm not in love with Mark. I don't think I ever was. But even so, it's no fun being rejected."

"Of course not." Relief swamped him, but Cam fought through it. This wasn't about him, it was about Deborah.

"I could deal with an impersonal kind of rejection." She stared at his aquarium, but Cam knew she wasn't seeing any fish. "You know, the *I'm not ready to get married* kind of thing." She slanted him a glance that commented, without words, on how familiar he himself must be with that phrase.

Cam winced.

"That's what I thought Mark meant," she said.

"Until today."

"Yes. Until I discovered he'd married someone else, which meant he'd rejected me, personally, and not marriage itself." Deborah drank some more of her coffee. "You know, you could at least have put some brandy or whiskey in this, so I'd have an excuse for blabbing my head off." She gave him a shadow of a grin.

"You don't need an excuse." He was missing something. A piece of the puzzle that would make everything, including the despair he'd thought he saw in her eyes, make sense. He could understand a certain amount of depression over being dumped. But if she wasn't in love with the guy—

"It's silly," Deborah said. "I should just forget about it. After all, everyone has to deal with rejection, don't they? I got over it when Rick left—he was my first serious boyfriend—and I'm already over Mark. It's bad luck, that's all. I just can't help thinking about it. And wondering if—'' she stopped and Cam saw her swallow ''—if maybe there's something lacking in me.''

''There is *nothing* lacking in you,'' Cam assured her. How had she gotten that idea? It wasn't as if ten men had rejected her. Only two.

And then he remembered his own conclusions about the rejection Deborah had suffered.

''I don't think this is about any of the guys you've dated.'' Cam waited until she looked at him. ''I think it's about your dad,'' he said gently.

Damned right it was. Her father's departure was the single thread running through the whole thing, connecting it all together.

She drew her brows together. ''My father?''

''Yes. I think you were at exactly the age when kids think everything that happens is about them. I think you decided your dad had rejected you.'' What an awful idea to get saddled with, too. Cam felt an unreasonable hostility toward her father for getting himself killed. Not to mention leaving Deborah in the first place.

Deborah shook her head. ''I know my dad left for reasons that had nothing to do with me. Of course I know that.''

''Intellectually, maybe. I'm talking about emotionally. I get the feeling you had a special bond with your father.''

Deborah sighed. ''As a child, I did. As a teenager?'' Her lips moved in a smile that held no humor. ''We were too much alike. Stubborn, among other things. I think that made him both proud and frustrated. Mostly frustrated in those last few months.''

Cam shook his head. ''I bet your dad was proud, more than anything else.''

''I don't know.'' Deborah shrugged. ''The last thing he heard from me was the slam of my bedroom door.'' Her head bent.

Cam's chest felt tight. ''Well, I hope you're not imagining that had anything to do with his leaving.''

She looked up. ''Of course not.'' But she said it just a little too quickly.

Cam gave her a faint smile. ''I bet you're wondering what the hell I could possibly know about it, aren't you? Well, all I know is this. When I was ten and my parents were yelling and screaming in divorce court, I figured it had to be my fault they hated each other so much. After all, I was the one they were fighting over, the reason they couldn't look at each other—or me—without coming apart at the seams.

''I was lucky, though, because the child advocate assigned to me was not only good with kids, she was also one hell of a psychologist. And she told it to me straight up—'Don't look to make any of this your fault. And don't ever judge yourself by what other people do, even if those people are your parents.'''

Deborah said nothing.

Cam held her gaze with his. ''You said your mother thinks your father would have come back. And she's probably right. But even if he had lived and never come back, it wouldn't make you any less terrific than you are. And just because two guys didn't have enough sense to value what they had with you doesn't make you any less wonderful, either.''

Deborah's eyes shifted. She opened her mouth and

closed it again. At any other time, the sight of a speechless Deborah would have given him a chuckle.

Right now he didn't feel like laughing.

"As I see it," Cam continued, "you've made a huge difference in a lot of children's lives. I'm not talking about the party, although I'm sure the kids will take away wonderful memories. I'm talking about the fact that you're there for them on a regular basis, giving your time, your energy and your generosity."

She lifted one shoulder in a self-conscious movement.

"You've changed me, too, you know." He smiled at her skeptical look. "It's true, I swear. Haven't I cut back on caffeine?"

Deborah snorted.

Cam laughed. "And don't forget charity work. I'd never gone beyond writing checks before, but getting personally involved is a lot more meaningful. I owe that experience to you." Gently he grasped her chin and forced her to look at him. "So judge yourself by what *you* do, okay?"

Deborah sat, still and silent. She looked as though she was thinking about it, though.

"I'm not trying to say your love life isn't important," Cam added, "only that it's just one facet of your life."

She nodded. A ghost of a smile crossed her lips. "Third time lucky, huh?"

Third time lucky.

Yeah. Except it was the unknown guy himself who'd be lucky as hell. He'd get to come home every night to the gutsy, laughing, bright-eyed Deborah. He'd get a woman as generous as she was cheerful.

Cam swallowed. He had to stop thinking about how right it felt having Deborah with him in his kitchen and in his house. Or how good it felt to laugh and enjoy the company of a woman who couldn't care less how much money he had.

He cleared his throat. "That's right. Third time lucky. You'll meet some great guy, and all the rest will be history."

"Yeah, maybe."

Cam raised a brow. "Hey, what's this? I expect a lot more conviction from you, Ms. Love-Conquers-All."

She shrugged. "Just because I believe in love doesn't mean I think it happens for everyone. For all I know, I'm not the type to inspire lasting feelings."

Cam stared at her. She believed what she was saying. He could see it in her eyes. Deborah actually believed she didn't inspire important feelings in men.

Cam closed his eyes. He didn't want to remember any of his own feelings about her. He didn't want to think about rightness or joy or laughter. He definitely didn't want to say it out loud, not right now and probably not ever. What he really wanted to do was deny it all.

But he couldn't do that. Because Deborah needed to hear it. She needed these truths a hell of a lot more than he needed to protect himself, his privacy or his pride.

Cam shifted to face her on the sofa. "That's complete bull, and to prove it, I'm going to tell you exactly how I feel about you."

He saw surprise flare in her vivid blue eyes, but he kept going. He had to build up some momentum or he might chicken out.

"You're my friend." Was the shock he felt about that in his voice? "You're the first woman I've had fun with since college. I think I could watch paint dry with you and still have a great time. Of course, you've got way too many opinions, and since you don't hold back any of them—"

She made a muffled noise that sounded like a snort, but Deborah was smiling.

He smiled back. "Like I said, you're my friend. The keeper kind, you know? The only woman friend I've ever had."

Cam stopped. How could he explain this next part, when he didn't even understand it himself? He stared down at his coffee table. "The confusing thing is, you're not only my friend, you're also the woman I'd most like to take to bed."

Her small intake of breath made Cam look at her. He saw shock and a strange emotion he couldn't identify.

Her mouth opened, so Cam held up a hand. It trembled and he quickly put it down again.

"I swear, I'm not trying to manipulate you into anything. We already came close to going to bed together, and you were right to back off. The only reason I'm telling you this now is that I think—" He cleared his throat. "Oh, hell, I'm bungling this."

"No. No, you're not." Her voice was uneven. "You're telling me this because you know just how rejected that news today made me feel." Her eyes had a sheen to them. "Don't ever let anyone convince you you're not a nice guy, Cameron Lyle."

"A Nice Guy? Me? *Never*." He pretended to shudder. "I'm not saying it to be nice. All I'm doing is reminding you that you're an incredibly desirable woman." He couldn't think about how desirable she was, or else he'd forget all about his vow to keep his hands off her.

"Thanks." Her voice held a husky note. This time he couldn't read the expression in her eyes, because her long lashes had dropped down to shield them.

"I'm not finished yet." In the quiet room, his pulse beat loudly. Every instinct he had screamed that he should be finished, that he *should* stop right there. After all, he'd already reassured her on the basic points, hadn't he? Why get into the messy stuff? Why make himself even more vulnerable?

Because he had to.

"I don't have any trouble at all with the friends part." He hesitated. "The passion stuff gets trickier."

Hell, yes. One look into her luminous eyes and he was drowning. He wanted to pull her into his arms so badly it was killing him.

But he had to stay on track. Cam drew in a breath deep enough to hurt his lungs. "I've always been so hung up on my privacy, you know? Especially with the women I date. I don't bring them home with me. I definitely don't cook dinner with them. But you..." He shook his head. "I actually want you around. And although I also just plain *want* you every time I look at you, I can handle that."

Once again, Cam couldn't meet her eyes, so this time he stared at his aquarium. The fish were swimming around and around and around. Just like him. This was all even harder to say than he'd thought.

Cut to the chase, Lyle.

God only knew what Deborah was thinking. She wasn't saying anything, and he sure as hell couldn't turn and look at her, so he might as well just finish what he'd started.

"Here's the part that really blows me away. Earlier this evening we were hanging out together in the kitchen. We were drinking our wine, talking, working on dinner. And I caught myself thinking what a drag it is that I don't believe the whole happily-ever-after thing is possible."

Cam swallowed, but his throat still felt tight. He took a breath. "The simple fact is, you're the only woman who's ever made me wish I believed in love."

Chapter Fourteen

Why was she crying? Because her dad was dead? Because she'd lost him twice and she missed him still? Because she was so afraid she was unlovable?

Or was she crying because Cameron obviously valued her enough to question, and even regret, his own convictions about love and marriage?

Deborah had no idea. But then, she didn't understand most of what had happened today, so at least she was consistent. Besides, it didn't matter right now. At this moment, nothing mattered except the feel of Cameron's arms close around her.

He cradled her against him and rocked her while the tears flooded out of her. He didn't murmur useless words or try to get her to stop crying. He simply sat there with her, holding her in a silent comfort that did more than anything he could have said.

His arms felt so good, so *right*. Deborah wanted to cry in them a lot longer, but she finally managed to pull herself together. For a few blissful seconds she rested against him, exhausted, listening to the steady beat of his heart and taking comfort from the feel of his very solid chest. Then she pulled back and ran a hand across her eyes.

"Sorry," she muttered, avoiding his gaze. "I've soaked your shirt." She must look a complete mess. Her face felt hot, and she was probably going to have a wicked headache.

"That's okay. I've got other shirts in my closet." The gentleness in his voice made her chest hurt.

"I don't usually cry in response to compliments." She gave him a crooked smile.

He didn't return it. "You've had an upsetting day. You probably needed a good cry."

"Maybe." And then the touching things he'd said to her had finished her off. But Deborah didn't mention that. She just looked at Cameron, and the knowledge of what it must have cost him to say those things reverberated inside her. Maybe that knowledge showed in her eyes, because faint color tinged his cheeks.

I want you every time I look at you.

You're the only woman who's ever made me wish I believed in love.

And here she'd been thinking he didn't desire her anymore.

Deborah met Cameron's vivid green gaze. "Thanks for making me feel better."

His sudden bark of laughter caught them both by surprise.

She laughed, too. "No, really, I do feel better. I know I look worse, but I'm not depressed anymore."

She was a lot of things, but depressed wasn't one of them. Back in her apartment, alone and in the quiet, she would bring out all the confusing, conflicting emotions and examine them as closely as she dared. But she couldn't do it now.

"Come on," Cameron said quietly, standing up. "I'll drive you home."

That wasn't what she wanted. Deborah didn't have to think long to know it. She didn't have the energy left to hide it from herself, either.

She wanted to stay right here with Cameron. She wanted to show him all the things she couldn't put into words. Most of all, she wanted to give, and receive, a gift that seemed way overdue.

Deborah drew a breath. "I'd rather stay with you." She sank back a little deeper into the sofa cushions.

Cameron shook his head. "That's not a good idea."

"Why not?"

His eyes were shuttered, unreadable. "Because if you stay, I don't think I—" He stopped. More color crept into his cheeks. "I'm not sure I can control myself," he muttered.

Shock waves hit her. Then came exhilaration mixed with a strange tenderness. Deborah smiled. "Ditto."

His indrawn breath sounded loud in the silence of the room. For long seconds, they stared at each other and neither of them said anything.

Then he let out a breath, and it sounded almost as loud on the exhale. "We should, though." He cleared his throat. "Control ourselves, I mean."

"Why?" She watched him move away from her, as if he figured physical distance would help.

"Because you're not—" Cameron shook his head. For the first time since she'd met him, he looked unsure of himself. "You're not yourself," he finished quietly. "You're off-balance, and I can't take advantage of that."

She chuckled. "You know something? Right now

I feel more balanced than I've felt in a long time."
It was true. She felt lighter, freer, as if life had suddenly become much simpler.

The passion stuff gets trickier.

Yet for her that wasn't true. Maybe because theirs was an honest passion, a friendly passion, an emotion she could never regret.

Deborah got up from the sofa. As she reached Cameron, she saw him swallow.

"Don't do anything you're going to regret," he warned.

His apparent lack of enthusiasm might have fazed her if she hadn't seen his eyes slowly catch fire as he looked at her.

"No regrets," Deborah said, and reached for him. She touched her lips to his and felt the contact in every nerve.

He held back. She could feel his restraint, his hesitation. Then he groaned. "This is insane." His answering kiss held desperation and desire in equal measures.

Deborah's lips moved under his. Joy filled her. Finally, finally, Cameron was kissing her again. He tasted like coffee and chocolate, only better. He tasted like all the excitement and all the passion she could ever want.

He tasted like Cameron.

Her tongue met his and a shiver went through her. She could feel the pounding of her heart. Or was it his? Impossible to know, as closely wrapped together as they were. She could feel his hard chest through her thin sweatshirt and was starkly aware that she'd gone braless.

As if he'd just discovered that fact, Cameron

nudged her sweatshirt aside and touched gentle fingers to her breast. He cupped the weight of it in his palms. She arched. The warmth and slight roughness of his hand was so exciting she almost couldn't stand it. Her breath was trapped somewhere in her throat.

More. She wanted more.

She met his gaze and for a long moment they stared at each other. And then they were at each other's clothes, tugging at zippers, pulling at buttons, hands feverish and eager. Deborah felt smooth skin, hard muscles, crisp curls. She pulled back to look.

He had a beautiful body. Hard, fit, still slightly tanned. He was tall and well muscled, but in an elegant, streamlined way. Deborah felt awed by so much masculine beauty.

Cameron liked her body, too. She could tell. His gaze roamed over her with an intensity and a passion that made her breath catch and her blood sing in her veins.

He led her up the stairs to his bedroom, where she caught only a glimpse of a hunter-green bedspread before he whipped it off. Then she was on the bed with him, deposited there with great care and eagerness.

Cameron's hand moved slowly down her body, lingering along the way. "You're beautiful." His voice was a husky murmur.

"No." But the wonder in his eyes made her feel as if she was.

"Yes. I can't believe you're here." He cleared his throat. "If you're going to change your mind, you'd better do it now."

"I'm not changing my mind." Deborah swept one hand down his chest in a leisurely movement.

His gasp and the tightening of his body thrilled her. Cameron's obvious pleasure at her touch made her own excitement even more acute.

The sudden touch of his lips on the tip of her breast sent fire streaking through her. His tongue caressed her until she was twisting beneath him. Then his dark head moved further down her body. Deborah captured it, held it, as he explored every inch of her with a concentration that touched her as much as it drove her wild. A whimper fought its way out of her throat.

Now, now.

As if he heard the words, Cameron took her face in his hands. His gaze searched hers, and she knew he saw only certainty there. She was touched that he looked for it. She was equally touched by his quick use of a small foil packet.

Then he kissed her again, a long, slow, deep kiss that went on and on, until all her insides felt like they were melting. She forgot everything except Cameron. His taste, his touch, his scent. Woodsy. Musky. Male.

Wonderful.

His fingers twined with hers. Resting on powerful forearms, he merged with her, slowly, deeply, his gaze holding hers the entire time. His eyes were a bright, glowing green, so beautiful she wanted to cry again.

Instead Deborah moved with him, meeting each stroke, rising and falling, awed by Cameron's strength and gentleness, amazed at how right it felt to be with him.

The power of her release hit her all at once, in flashes and pulses and gasps of wonder. Dimly, she heard Cameron moan as he found his own release.

When it was over, she lay in a damp tangle with

him, her head on his shoulder, floating in a warm contentment.

And then she slept.

HE WAS AN IDIOT.

From his deck, Cam stared out at the purple blackness of the night sky. A thin sliver of a moon was the only light, since his own darkened house obscured the lights of what few neighbors he had. He leaned on the deck rail and watched the clouds do a slow drift past the moon. In the distance an owl hooted.

He was worse than an idiot. He was a hypocrite. He'd promised himself he would leave Deborah alone, and he'd broken that promise. Worst of all, he'd done it at a time when she was especially vulnerable. How was she going to feel about their lovemaking when she woke up in the morning? Would he see regret in her eyes?

Tonight she'd been more vulnerable than he'd ever seen her before, and it was his fault. All he'd accomplished with his pathetic little confession binge was to make Deborah feel worse.

She'd denied it, of course. She'd claimed she wasn't depressed anymore, but then she would say that, wouldn't she? As he'd noticed before, she was a generous person. She knew he was trying to make her feel better, and she wouldn't want him to guess he'd done just the opposite. He'd probably embarrassed her, too. In all likelihood, he'd given Deborah details she'd rather not know.

You're the only woman who's ever made me wish I believed in love.

Cam winced. The next time he got the urge to be

that honest, he'd hit himself over the head with a two-by-four until the urge left him.

But as uncomfortable as his confessions made him, they weren't a crime. Taking Deborah to bed had been the real crime. He'd known damned well even as he did it that he shouldn't. He'd known it and been unable to stop himself.

The crazy thing was that, even though he knew it was wrong, making love to Deborah hadn't *felt* wrong. It had felt wonderful. Incredible. Soul-strengthening. It had felt completely right, and even now, at three in the morning with guilt hammering him, it still felt that way.

Idiot.

Cam shivered. He was cold, in spite of the mildness of the damp spring air. He could smell that dampness and, mixed in with it, the rich smoke from a neighbor's fireplace.

He'd probably ruined his relationship with Deborah.

It wasn't a new thought. Even as he'd taken her in his arms, he'd warned himself not to risk their relationship. He'd ignored the warning, and now the thought of the damage he'd done made all his insides tense up.

Six months ago, he would never have used the word *relationship* before he'd slept with the woman in question. But then, six months ago he'd had no idea he could feel such a...a *bond* with a woman. He would never have imagined he could say to anyone what he'd said to Deborah. And he would definitely never have fought the desire to make love to a woman, knowing even as he fought that the only reason he held back was that he couldn't risk losing what he had with her. He'd never before had anything important enough to be worried about losing it.

But if he wasn't careful, he would screw everything up with Deborah. He didn't do lasting physical involvement. That meant the only way to have a lasting relationship with her was to stay friends.

Period.

Cam grimaced. All he could do now was major damage control. He had to tell Deborah the full truth, and above all, he had to make it clear that he wasn't rejecting her. He couldn't do that to Deborah.

Although his business trip next week felt like bad timing, it was probably all for the best. When he came back, he'd go to the Kids First party and take the lighthearted approach. He would laugh and joke, and Deborah would be relieved. After all, in spite of her temporary insanity tonight, she knew as well as he did, maybe better, that anything but friendship between them would be a bust. Much as he hated to admit it, she'd had him pegged from the beginning.

With one final shiver Cam crossed the deck and headed inside. He'd do everything possible to put their relationship back on the old footing. Because although he knew very little else for sure, he did know one thing.

He couldn't lose Deborah.

SWEETNESS AND LIGHT had just closed for the day, but its huge kitchen smelled like a chapter out of Deborah's childhood. Every favorite party food item she could remember crowded the steel counters. She knew that still more food filled the huge freezer and refrigerator, but since those goodies were hidden, she only had to deal with them in the abstract. It was the huge platters of brownies and cupcakes that worried her.

"I've never seen so much food in my life," Deborah said.

Ann grimaced. "Yes, well, its status as food is debatable, but I'll grant you there's a lot of it. Amazing what a hundred and twenty children can put away."

Deborah knew from experience how much food a mere dozen children could go through. It *was* amazing.

"Looks like everything's under control here." She grinned at her friend. "I want you to know I appreciate all your time and energy, not to mention the sacrifice of your culinary standards. Thanks for your devotion to the cause."

"You're welcome. Glad to help."

"Are you going to bring Sheldon?" She'd like to meet the pharmacist Ann was dating.

"No. We broke up on Wednesday. Just as well, too." She grimaced. "He was always worried about what his mother wanted him to do." Ann paused. "Speaking of breakups, are you really okay about Mark getting married?"

Deborah almost said *Who?* She gathered her scattered thoughts together. "Yes." In the wake of last Friday night, it was hard to think about anyone but Cameron.

Cameron, comforting her. Cameron, kissing her. Cameron, showing her with passionate eyes and body just how powerful lovemaking could be.

Cameron, driving her home the next morning while silence hung heavily between them.

She'd woken up to find the bed empty and Cameron in the kitchen, fixing eggs, bacon, pancakes and hash browns. Neither his smile nor his gentle teasing about her sound sleep disguised the circles under his eyes. He obviously hadn't slept well. Which had to mean he regretted making love with her.

Except that was clearly not true. Even if the banked desire in his eyes hadn't made that fact clear, his explanation after breakfast would have. And Deborah couldn't disagree with anything he said. Their friendship *was* important. His track record *was* abysmal. Confused but also warmed by Cameron's obvious affection, Deborah had returned his smile, followed his lead and promised herself she'd figure it all out later.

Ann was a blur of movement as she closed down the kitchen, putting the last trays of perishable items in the huge fridge and checking to make sure everything was properly plastic wrapped. "I'm glad you're okay with it," she said. "I mean, you did say you're over Mark, and I believe you, but sometimes depression sneaks up and bites you on the butt, you know what I mean?"

Deborah nodded. That was probably a good description for what had happened to her last Friday before Cameron had shown up at her door. But since her evening—and night—with him, she'd uncovered a lot of different emotions. She hadn't figured out all of them yet, even though it seemed like she'd spent the whole week doing nothing but thinking.

She'd started with the safer emotions, like gratitude. Cameron had reassured her about herself as a person, so naturally she'd been grateful. Who wouldn't be? She'd felt warmth and affection toward him, too, especially when he'd admitted he liked having her around. After all, she enjoyed Cameron's company, and she missed him when he wasn't there.

She'd missed him this week, even though she needed the chance to think without getting distracted.

Not quite so safe an emotion was the relief she'd felt at the discovery that Cameron still desired her. That was harder to admit, especially since they had tacitly agreed that Friday night's lovemaking would not be repeated. She shouldn't want passionate feelings from a man she'd been so determined to resist.

And then there was the single sentence she couldn't get out of her head. *You're the only woman who's ever made me wish I believed in love.*

Every time those words echoed in her mind, grief and a sharp sense of loss assailed her. These were the emotions she didn't understand. Where were they coming from? And why did she sense that the answer to that question hovered just beyond her reach, like a word that remained stubbornly on the tip of her tongue?

"Deborah?" Ann was waving a hand in front of her face.

She started. "Sorry. I spaced out for a minute there."

Her friend smiled. "I guess you're allowed, considering how hard you've worked to put this event together. I just wanted to verify that we're still on the original timetable for food service."

"We are. No changes." Deborah gathered up her purse and all her various lists and prepared to leave Ann in peace.

"I assume you're coming with Cameron?"

The mere sound of his name made her heart skip a beat, and how ridiculous was that?

Deborah shook her head. "I have to be there early for setup, and in any case, Cameron's out of town all week on business and will barely get back in time, so he's coming straight to the party.''

Her stomach felt jittery every time she thought about seeing him again. If only she could get those images out of her head. The ones that circled around and around in her mind like continuous reel footage.

Cameron, staring at her, his eyes filled with passion. Cameron, lowering his head to kiss her. Cameron, his powerful, naked shoulders rising above her as he claimed her. Cameron, flushed and groaning with pleasure.

Deborah closed her eyes. How was she ever going to look at the man again and think *friend* instead of *lover?* How could she laugh and joke with him when the mere thought of him made her mouth dry up and her hands shake?

One thing was for sure. She'd better pull herself together, because tomorrow she'd have to face him again with all the memories of last Friday night hanging between them.

Heaven help her.

DEBORAH DUG AROUND in her closet. She had shoes somewhere, black pumps that would be perfect with her dress. All she had to do was find them. Which would be simple enough if she didn't have so much junk in this closet. She should have hunted them down before now, a mere hour before the party.

She reached into the very back of the closet and found a shoebox.

Bingo.

Except there were no shoes inside. Only a photograph, framed in pewter.

Deborah stared down at her father and herself. Both

laughing, caught in midstride at the father-daughter dance at her junior high school. It was the last photo taken before he died. One look and she was there again, surrounded by lights and laughter, touching the rough silk of her dad's suit jacket, inhaling the scents of his citrus aftershave and the rose corsage he'd given her.

Deborah studied his face. Such a familiar face, even now. Blue eyes, just like hers. A wide grin. And that small lock of hair that always escaped, falling over his forehead. She'd been so proud of her dad, who was tall and handsome instead of paunchy like so many of the other fathers. Her dad, the scientist who did important and sometimes secret work.

Her dad, who had a booming laugh and a contagious joy in living.

Her dad, who'd loved his family above everything else.

Her dad, who'd understood her because they were so much alike.

Throat tightening, Deborah stared at the photo.

Surely he'd seen, just as she could see in this picture she held, the love shining in her face? Surely he'd seen beyond slammed doors, huffy sighs and the self-absorption of a teenager? He had to have known how important, how *necessary,* he was to her.

You're so stubborn, Deborah. Her father's voice, filled with exasperation.

Thud. Her bedroom door, slamming shut.

Deborah blinked once, hard. She took a long, slow breath.

Of course he'd known.

Cameron was right. Rick and Mark weren't the real issue at all. Her father was. But he hadn't rejected her, not intentionally. He'd been stressed out, depressed and confused, and his problems had nothing to do with her or with anything she should or shouldn't have done.

Slowly Deborah took the photo out of the shoebox. She dusted it off and arranged it on her nightstand. Then she went back into the closet to find her shoes and started dressing for the party, wishing her hands would stop trembling. Wishing she could stop thinking about seeing Cameron again, but knowing it was a useless wish. He was always there, occupying a corner of her mind.

Cameron.

Deborah sat down on her bed so suddenly and awkwardly that she almost put a run in her new pair of hose. Then she stared, unseeing, at the wall. How could she have missed it for so long? How could she have been so dense?

She was in love with Cameron.

She'd fallen so deeply in love with him there was no chance of her ever falling out. She loved a man who, although he wished otherwise, did not believe in love.

Deborah closed her eyes. This revelation certainly explained the grief she'd been trying to figure out, but discovering the cause of it didn't bring her the relief she'd expected.

Somehow, in spite of every effort she'd made not to form an emotional attachment to the man, she'd managed to do it anyway. And honestly, how the heck was she supposed to have stopped herself? It wasn't enough that she'd found out he had a sense of humor and more generosity in him than she could ever have guessed. No, she'd had to also discover his compassion and understanding.

From the second she realized how much he'd done for her during her bout with the flu, she should have kissed her heart goodbye, because that was probably when she'd lost it. How was she supposed to resist that kind of caring?

And then there were his kisses. And his lovemaking. The thought of that made her legs go weak. Heat spread to every corner of her body. And every time she thought about what would happen if he made love to her again...

Deborah flinched. *Don't think about it.*

If she hadn't already been a goner, she'd have fallen in love with him Friday night, when he'd sacrificed his own interests to make her feel better. It had worked, too. How could she doubt her own worth when Cameron had such strong feelings for her and freely admitted to them?

Deborah frowned. Cameron hadn't needed to admit that she made him want to believe in love, though. They'd argued so often about that topic, and she'd always had the impression he was glad he didn't believe in love, that his lack of belief in some way reassured him that he was making the right choices in life.

So why had he admitted a wish like that to her? To make her feel better? No, he'd already accomplished that.

He clearly hadn't said it to get her into bed, either. That wasn't his style, and in any case, Cameron had been all set to take her home until she'd pressed the issue.

So what was she supposed to do now? Admit defeat and slink away? After all, if the many gorgeous, sophisticated women who'd pursued Cameron had failed to change his thinking, who was she to expect she could accomplish something they hadn't?

For long moments Deborah traced the pattern on her bedspread and thought. Finally she lifted her head. After Friday night, she knew exactly who she was to Cameron Lyle.

She was the woman he saw as a person and liked.

She was the woman he desired so much his hands shook when he made love to her.

And most importantly, she was the woman who made him wish he could throw away beliefs he'd carried with him for a lifetime.

He'd told her all these things himself. But there was one thing Cameron hadn't needed to tell her.

If you want something badly enough, you have to get out there and fight for it.

Chapter Fifteen

Cam gazed around the huge gymnasium. Artistically draped streamers and ribboned bunches of brightly colored helium balloons were everywhere. It was the birthday party to top all birthday parties.

And he was late for it.

Damn.

Never mind that there was a logical, and unavoidable, reason for his tardiness. Reasons didn't change the fact that he'd missed more than half of the party Deborah had worked so hard to plan. Fortunately, he'd gotten here in time to take care of his duties at the basketball toss.

But first he had to find Deborah.

Deborah, who he'd missed like hell all week. Deborah, who was probably royally steamed at him for being so late.

Deborah, who suddenly stood ten feet away wearing the red dress he'd bought her.

She was gorgeous. The red silk skimmed lightly over her, nipping in at her small waist and flowing over slender hips and thighs to end just above her knees. Her hair was a mass of thick, shining gold waves that framed bright eyes and pink cheeks. She wore only a little makeup, and that was all she needed.

Cam's breath caught. One look at her and his brain stopped functioning. His body worked fine, though. His heart was pounding so hard he was afraid—even convinced—that everyone could hear it. His blood raced through him, hot and hectic.

He focused again on the red dress.

"You wore it." Cam felt like that was a sign of something, but he didn't know what. He couldn't stop smiling.

Deborah smiled back. "Yes."

"My flight was delayed. Engine trouble."

She nodded. He could tell she hadn't assumed the worst, that she'd been confident he would come. Her faith was in her smile, and it warmed him.

Cam cleared his throat. "The decorations all look great." True, but it was Deborah his eyes couldn't get enough of. It seemed like a month since he'd seen her, not a week. Could she tell how badly he wanted to ignore the masses of people around them and sweep her into his arms?

"Thanks." Was that an answering desire in her eyes?

Don't go there, Lyle. Think friends.

"I, uh, guess I'd better get over to the basketball hoop." Cam took one more long look at her. It felt like there were two conversations going on here, and the one that really mattered had no words in it at all.

"Yes," Deborah agreed.

"I'll talk to you later."

She nodded.

Just then, a tiny dark-haired girl, wearing a frilly pink dress and a chocolate-smeared smile, threw herself into Deborah's arms. Cam watched Deborah's face light up. Joy shone in her smile as she hugged and kissed the child, and suddenly his mind filled with a different image, an image of Deborah and a toddler with blond hair and delicate features just like her own.

Unlike you, I'm not afraid of marriage.

Of course she wasn't. Deborah would get married and have kids. Some other guy's kids.

Cam stood, rooted to the spot. His vision went funny, as if he were looking through a tunnel. Every other sound faded away, until all he could hear was the blood pounding in his ears. He felt way too hot, except for the small bead of cold sweat trickling down his temple.

A moment later he turned and fled to the basketball court.

FROM THE COMPARATIVE safety of the toddler frog toss, Deborah flicked a glance toward the basketball hoop. The sand art booth stood between them, but it didn't matter, because she could still feel Cameron's gaze. His eyes did his talking for him, and they were just as intent as they'd been last Friday night. Except this time, she wasn't at all confident about what they were saying to her.

What if she was wrong?

Deborah shivered. It was a good thing helping toddlers toss a beanbag frog into the "pond" wasn't a thought-intensive proposition. Because her brain was down for the count and had been ever since she'd first suspected that desire wasn't the only thing she saw in Cameron's eyes.

Was she imagining it? Had she conjured it up because she wanted to see it so badly?

No. She was right. She had to be. She was right on target.

And then, quite suddenly, she was mad, too. Every syllable of his gentle, *friendly* talk with her last Saturday morning echoed in her mind, and she was more furious than she'd ever been in her life.

Deborah barely heard the emcee announce the end of the party. Confetti drifted down from the ceiling, and more squeals of excitement broke out. She handed over the last toddler prize, but she only had one thought.

Cameron.

Before she knew it, Deborah was at the basketball toss, confronting him. Even in shirtsleeves, his dark hair dotted with confetti, he was dangerously attractive. Her pulse rate kicked up several notches.

Which only made her madder.

"We have to talk. *Now.*"

Cameron stared at her.

Deborah looked around the gymnasium. The place was total bedlam, kids running around, balloons popping, streamers and confetti everywhere. Although the party was officially over, there had to be at least eighty people of assorted ages milling around.

"Right now?" His wary expression told her he understood they weren't going to talk about the weather.

"Yes, now." Deborah grabbed his hand. A sudden idea came to her even as she pulled him out of the gym and into the hallway. Halfway down it she stopped, opened a green door and gave him a gentle push through it. She closed it behind her with a small slam that echoed in the room.

"It's pitch-black in here." His neutral, careful tone

might have made her laugh, if tension weren't pressing in on her until she wanted to scream.

And if she weren't so damned mad at Cameron.

And if she weren't so scared.

Deborah yanked a chain, and a single bare bulb lit up the janitor's closet. She saw Cameron glance around. Cleaning supplies of every description filled the floor-to-ceiling shelves. Brooms and mops hung on the far wall. A vacuum cleaner occupied one corner of the small room.

Not exactly the most auspicious place for this discussion, but what the heck. Nothing mattered except getting this settled, once and for all.

Her tension must have communicated itself, because Cameron barely gave their surroundings a glance. His gaze locked on her face.

Deborah glared at him. "It's too late for this *friends only* thing. Maybe it always was, but it's definitely too late now. I don't care how reasonable you made it sound last Saturday. It's a total crock, and I can't believe I bought into it even for a second." The words spilled out of her so fast she could barely get in a breath. But she couldn't seem to stop herself.

"We can't go back to being only friends. I realize you don't want to hear that. I know you'd rather tell yourself fairy tales about our friendship being too important to risk, but that's too damned bad. I'm not going to settle for only friendship with you when I know we could have something so much better, so much stronger, if you only had the guts to admit it." She drew a breath that hurt her lungs.

Cameron's eyes held shock. Deborah looked away. She fixed her gaze on a bright yellow broom and wished she could stop her hands from shaking.

"I've been a total mess all week. My thoughts just went around and around until I thought I'd go insane. I've never been so confused in my life," she told him. "And no wonder, with you blowing first hot, then cold."

"I didn't—"

"Yes, you did," she retorted, pinning him with a stare. "What else do you call making love to me Friday night as if I were the only woman in the world for you, and then telling me Saturday morning that our friendship is too important to ruin with something as trivial as sex?"

His jaw clenched. "That is *not* what I said."

"Maybe not, but it's what you meant, and you had me so confused I could barely see straight, never mind make any sense out of what I was feeling. That's probably why it took me so long to realize I'd fallen in love with you."

Cameron's eyes blazed. His mouth opened, but Deborah put her hand over it.

"No, don't say anything," she said fiercely. "Hear me out. You feel something for me, something besides friendship and lust. You *have* to. I should have figured it out as soon as you told me things I know you didn't really want to say."

She took a quick breath. "Look, I realize you've been telling yourself for years that love, romantic love, doesn't exist. I also know you've had strong personal reasons for believing that. *But you're wrong.* What's more, I think you know it. You said I'm your friend, that you want me around all the time, that you could have fun watching paint dry with me and that you want to take me to bed." She swallowed.

"Yes." His eyes were greener than she'd ever seen them. "And—"

"No, wait. Let me finish. That's exactly how I feel about you. And that's what romantic love is all about. It's like a very passionate friendship. Tell me something, Cameron. Why did you go that extra mile and admit to me that I make you want to believe in love?"

He didn't answer. He just stared at her.

She stared back. "You don't know, do you?"

"No."

"Okay, I'll tell you. I think when you said that to me you were really telling me not to give up on you. I think you want very badly to believe in love, and in my experience, wanting something badly enough is more than half the battle. For both our sakes, you'd better pull together all the courage I know you have and *just do it*. Really, you have no choice."

Deborah took a deep breath. Oh, God, she was scared. But she had to keep going. She had to make him see.

Besides, rejection was a small risk to take for a lifetime of happiness.

"I know you don't want to hear this, but you're going to, anyway," she said. "Over the past few weeks you've given me all the proof I need. You can run, but you can't hide. You can swear up and down denying it, but it won't change a thing." Deborah jabbed one shaking index finger at him for emphasis. "You, Mr. Cameron Lyle, are in love with me."

Silence, long and loud, echoed in the closet. Deborah listened to her heart pound and almost missed his reply.

"I know," Cameron said.

IN THE SILENCE of the janitor's closet Cam watched the changing expressions on Deborah's face.

"You know?" she echoed finally.

Cam smiled. She sounded shell-shocked. She looked as if she was going to crumple up in a heap any second. Which was all the excuse he needed to pull her into his arms, as he'd been dying to do for days now.

Her lips met his, opening immediately, so warm and moist that Cam groaned. She speared her fingers through his hair, sending a shiver of desire through him. Her hips rubbed against his with enough passion to make him wish they were anywhere but here.

A broom closet, for God's sake.

"You love me?" she said when they finally came up for air.

"Yes." He chuckled. He felt suddenly light and free, almost giddy. Deborah loved him. And he loved her. "Did you really think I wouldn't figure it out?"

She smiled. "I knew I didn't want to wait ten years."

"Cynic."

Deborah laughed.

"I should have realized it much sooner." Cam gave a wry smile. Yeah, like when he couldn't bring himself to seduce her. Or when he'd gotten jealous, which was completely unlike him. Or when he'd put Deborah's needs ahead of his own. "But I finally figured it out when I saw you with a little girl. I don't know her name, but she was wearing a frilly pink dress and she came up to you and gave you a big hug and a kiss—"

"Lauren," said Deborah.

"—and I could see you hugging and kissing your

own child some day. I remember thinking it would
be some other guy's kid, and I knew I couldn't let
that happen, that I loved you and had to marry you
myself." He shook his head. "I think I almost fainted
then."

"You fainted at the idea of marrying me?" Deborah arched her brows at him. She lowered them
again immediately. "Darn it, I've got to stop doing
that eyebrow trick of yours."

"Why? It looks cute on you," he teased.

"When we first met, you didn't think there was
anything cute about me at all," she reminded him.

"Yes, I did."

She shook her head. "You scowled at me all the
time."

"You were engaged! Every time I saw that ring of
yours, it drove me nuts. Besides that, I was sure you
were way too young for me." Cam grinned. "And
even once those problems were sorted out, I knew we
were still wrong for each other. That's why I invited
you to go to all those events with me."

"I knew it! You figured I was a safe choice—"

"*Safe?* You've got to be kidding! I was way too
attracted to you. My plan was to get you out of my
system by letting your chatter drive me up the wall."

Deborah looked affronted. "Like I said, I only
chatter when I'm nervous."

"So I discovered. At which point I decided I'd
have to seduce you instead." Which hadn't worked
either, of course. Making love with her had only made
him want her more. He smiled. Good thing he'd have
a lifetime to cure himself of her, since that was what
it would take.

Deborah punished him by giving him a long, sultry

kiss, her mouth eager and so seductive Cam felt his heart rate shoot up. He couldn't stop himself from touching her breasts through the thin silk of her dress.

She moaned.

"We've got to get out of here," he muttered.

Deborah pulled her mouth away and shook her head. "Not so fast." She smiled. "I still haven't recovered from shock."

"I'm not sure I ever will." He grinned back at her. "But then, I've had several huge surprises lately. For example, only recently I realized that where you're concerned, I have an endless capacity for jealousy."

"Jealousy?"

He nodded. "Remember that yuppie guy at the party? Justin?"

"Jason. I was never interested in him."

"Maybe not, but he was damned interested in you. And I was stunned at how mad that made me." Cam eyed her mouth. It looked too tempting to resist.

He lowered his head. Her lips parted under his and he savored the taste of her, the feel of her. She was warm and enticing, and she'd clearly missed him this week, too. Probably nowhere near as much as he'd missed her, but her eagerness sent a thrill through him. His trousers were uncomfortably tight, and he hadn't even touched her yet.

Oh, God, he had to touch her. Just for a minute.

Gently Cam manoeuvered Deborah until she was leaning against the wall. Then he unzipped the back of her dress, slipped its tiny straps off her shoulders and unfastened her bra.

"Cam," she sighed.

Once he was touching her he couldn't seem to stop. Cam ran his hands over her soft, warm skin. Her back, her arms, her neck, her breasts. He loved the feel of her. She smelled like a spring garden, light and subtle. He bent his head and took one hardened nipple into his mouth.

Deborah gasped.

The tiny noise sounded incredibly erotic. His heart pounding, Cam rubbed the lower half of his body, hard and aching, against hers. Her legs twined around his and her hands held his mouth to her breast. He wanted to rip the rest of that dress off Deborah. He wanted to drive himself into her. He wanted to make her scream with joy.

But they were in a damned *closet.*

With a groan, Cam wrenched his mouth away.

He gasped for breath. "We've really, *really* got to get out of here."

Deborah pulled out of his arms. "You're right." The little panting breaths she took almost sent him over the edge. "The cleanup crew will be headed this way any second." With hands that shook, she refastened her bra and adjusted the bodice of her dress.

Cam took a careful breath. "Please tell me you're not on the cleanup crew."

"That's right, I'm not."

"Thank God."

"Of course, I am in charge of the entire event," she reminded him. "Which means I've got to make sure all the loose ends are tied up."

Cam closed his eyes. Then he sighed. "At least it's a good cause."

"The best."

Cam concentrated on ignoring his clamoring body. "I bet you'd be great at planning fund-raisers. Maybe you should do some of that after we're married."

Deborah gave him a hesitant look. "You know, we don't have to get married, at least not right now. Just knowing you love me is incredibly terrific. We could ease into marriage slowly—"

"No." Cam shook his head. "I don't have any doubts. And I want a family, preferably before I get too much longer in the tooth. Don't you?"

"Of course I do. A big, happy family."

He shot her a wary look. "How big a family?"

Deborah grinned at him. "Oh, I think three or four kids should do it, don't you?"

"Sounds good to me."

"Plus assorted pets, of course." She gave a sudden chuckle.

"What's funny?" Cam's gaze roamed over her face. She was so beautiful. And she was his.

"I was just thinking how excited Libby will be to share living quarters with your fish," Deborah said.

Cam stared at her and felt the blood drain out of his face. "Oh, no." He put his hand to his forehead and took a long, steadying breath. "Okay. I guess there's only one solution. I'll have to give away my fish."

"No, you won't." Deborah patted him on the back. "Don't worry. We'll get a top for the tank so Libby can't get in there. She'll just have fun watching them." She gave him an innocent smile. "That's all I meant, you know."

"Yeah, right." Cam shook his head. "Living with you is going to give me a heart attack. When will you marry me?"

Deborah eyed him. "You know, you haven't asked me."

"I can remedy that right now." Cam got down on

one knee next to the huge floor-waxing machine. "Deborah Clark, will you do me the honor of becoming my wife?"

"With pleasure."

"Thank goodness for that!" yelled a voice beyond the door.

Deborah threw it open. In the hallway stood Barb and Ann. Beyond them was a group of women Cam assumed must be the rest of the cleanup crew. All wore beaming grins.

"I was afraid she'd turn you down and I'd have to resign," said Barb.

"I was afraid she'd insist, *yet again,* that she's not interested in you and I'd have to slap sense into her," said Ann.

Cam looked at Deborah. "Did you really tell her you weren't interested in me?"

Deborah gazed into his eyes. "Never mind about that," she murmured in a voice that sent his pulse skyrocketing once more. She turned to their interested audience. "See you later." Then she took Cam's hand and led him out of the closet. Together they ran down the hall and out the door to the parking lot.

On the other side of the door, cheers echoed loud and clear in the hallway.

Epilogue

One year later

"Great food, Ann, even better than last year's," Deborah said as she gave her friend a thumbs-up. Confetti drifted from the ceiling and children's laughter echoed through the gymnasium.

"Thanks. Although I still say calling this stuff food is overly complimentary." Her friend grinned. "What does Cameron think of your food preferences?"

Deborah laughed. "He's outlawed frozen dinners."

"Thank God."

"Except for keeping him company, I stay out of the kitchen, which suits us both fine."

Ann nodded. "You don't have time to cook, anyway. You've got too many fund-raisers to plan."

"True." She loved her work. And it was satisfying to be able to use her skills and experience to benefit charities. Kids First was still her favorite.

"Speaking of Cameron, where is that handsome husband of yours?"

"Helping Barb over at the photography booth." Deborah smiled. "She says he's good at getting the kids to sit still, but I think she mostly just loves having him as her assistant so she can boss him around.''

''I wonder how many times he's threatened to fire her?''

''Oh, dozens, I'm sure.''

They both laughed. For a few minutes Deborah stood quietly, absorbing the joyful chaos around her. In the nine months since she'd married Cam, her life had changed almost beyond recognition. She finally had the friend, lover and companion she'd wanted so badly. How had she gotten this lucky?

Yes, life was good, and soon it would be even better. Her throat tightened. Time to get Cam.

The second he and Barb finished photographing the last partygoer, Deborah grabbed his hand. ''Excuse us, Barb, but I need to talk to my husband.''

Barb shook her head. ''Uh-oh, what have you done, my boy?''

He raised his eyebrows at her. ''The party's over now, Barb, which means you're back to being *my* assistant again.''

She grinned. ''Darn, and I was just getting the hang of this boss thing, too.''

He shuddered.

Barb laughed. ''You know what your problem is? You're still miffed about losing our bet and having to pay me that fifty dollars.''

''Now that's where you're wrong.'' Cam put his arm around Deborah and looked down at her with an expression that put a lump in her throat. ''It's the best bet I ever lost.''

''Amen to that,'' said his assistant.

Deborah laughed. ''See you later, Barb.'' She

pulled Cam out of the gymnasium and halfway down the hallway, stopping in front of a green door.

"You know, I'm getting a strong sense of déjà vu, here," Cam said.

Deborah ushered him inside, yanked the light on and smiled at him. "I figure some traditions shouldn't be broken."

He stared at the floor-waxing machine, then shifted his gaze to Deborah. "Did you haul me in here to force a proposal out of me again?"

She laughed. "You are such an idiot." She could hear the love in her voice, and maybe Cam could, too, because he gave her a tender smile.

"Isn't that most of my charm?" he teased.

"No, most of your charm is that you're a wonderful husband." As she'd known he would be. When Cameron Lyle made a commitment, he took it seriously.

"You're going to be a wonderful father, too," Deborah said.

"Well, I hope so, since it's an important—" He stopped. Stared at her. "You mean...?"

She nodded. "We're going to have a baby." Smiling, she watched him.

Cam's eyes lit up. He pulled her to him, hugged her close and laughed out loud. "When?"

"In seven months. October." Deborah watched joy fill his eyes and wondered how life could get any better than this. Then Cam's mouth came down on hers, and she stopped thinking and gave herself up to his kiss.

Coming in December from

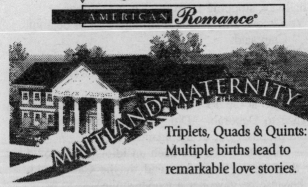

MAITLAND MATERNITY

Triplets, Quads & Quints:
Multiple births lead to
remarkable love stories.

When Maitland Maternity Hospital opens a new
multiple-birth wing donated by the McCallum family,
unforgettable surprises are sure to follow. Don't miss the
fun, the romance, the joy...as the McCallum triplets find
love just outside the delivery-room door.

Watch for:

TRIPLET SECRET BABIES
by Judy Christenberry
December 2001

QUADRUPLETS ON THE DOORSTEP
by Tina Leonard
January 2002

THE McCALLUM QUINTUPLETS
(3 stories in 1 volume)
featuring *New York Times* bestselling author Kasey Michaels,
Mindy Neff and Mary Anne Wilson
February 2002

Available at your favorite retail outlet.

HARLEQUIN®
Makes any time special ®

Visit us at www.eHarlequin.com

HARMAIT

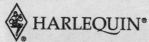

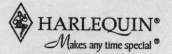

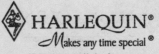